The Feester Filibuster

The Feester Filibuster

For Blair

a swimmingly good girl!

Molly Levite Griffis

Molly Levite Griffis

EAKIN PRESS ✠ Austin, Texas

To
Foster Harris
and
Harold Keith—

How I wish
they were here
to read it!

FIRST EDITION
Copyright © 2002
By Molly Griffis
Published in the United States of America
By Eakin Press
A Division of Sunbelt Media, Inc.
P.O. Drawer 90159 ☜ Austin, Texas 78709-0159
email: sales@eakinpress.com
🖥 website: www.eakinpress.com 🖥
ALL RIGHTS RESERVED.
1 2 3 4 5 6 7 8 9
1-57168-693-2 HB
1-57168-694-0 PB

Library of Congress Cataloging-in-Publication Data
Griffis, Molly Levite.
 The Feester filibuster / Molly Levite Griffis.
  p. cm.
Summary: The war declared by President Roosevelt after the bombing of Pearl Harbor in December, 1941, seems remote to fifth-grader John Alan until he finds out that his classmate Rachel thinks he is a spy for the Japanese and wants him deported to another country.
 ISBN 1-57168-693-2 — ISBN 1-57168-694-0 (pbk.)
 1. World War, 1939-1945–Oklahoma–Juvenile fiction. [1. World War, 1939-1945–Oklahoma–Fiction. 2. Interpersonal relations–Fiction. 3. Schools–Fiction. 4. Oklahoma–Fiction. 5. World War, 1939-1945–United States–Fiction.] I. Title.
PZ7.G88165 Fe 2002
[Fic]–dc21   2002008188

Contents

To be read by boys only!

(Girls not allowed to read this page!
Rachel Dalton, this means you!)

My name is John Alan Feester, and I just finished reading a book called *The Rachel Resistance*. It is about this redheaded girl named Rachel who talks all the time and thinks she knows everything. Since I am the guy Rachel was resisting, I think you need to hear what really happened. I know for a fact, however, that if somebody tries to tell a story, Rachel will start interrupting. So I decided to pull a filibuster.

Now, a filibuster is something those senators up in Washington, D.C. do all the time. It's where one person starts talking, and it's positively, absolutely against the rules for anybody else to interrupt. Ever. That's a filibuster.

Just in case you haven't read Rachel's version of

the war between the two of us, I will tell you what she says happened. I can do it in twenty-five words or less. (Those advertising jingle contests always have a "twenty-five words or less" rule. I entered one once. This was my jingle: "Slurp Lipton's Soup, Not the Other Goop!" Seven words! But I didn't win.)

Bet you a quarter I can say in twenty-five words or less what "motor mouth" Rachel took two hundred twenty-three pages to tell. Here goes:

"Pearl Harbor got bombed. Rachel thought John Alan did it. He did not."

If you took time to count the words (girls did, boys didn't, but girls are not supposed to be reading this!), you know that's a baker's dozen (thirteen) words so far. Add: "Rachel's best friend, Paul, who stole her pencil box, moved to California."

The whole book in twenty-five words exactly!

I win! But don't tell Rachel, okay? She gets really mad when I win.

Now turn the page for a new perspective on the events of *The Rachel Resistance*—the *right* one!

John Alan Feester

CHAPTER 1
December 14, 1941

"They're movin' the Rose Bowl?" John Alan Feester bellowed when he heard the news. He yelled it so loud a couple of first-grade boys playing marbles outside the window of Miss Mae Ella Cathcart's fifth-grade classroom heard him. They talked about what he said a minute and decided a Rose Bowl must be something you put flowers in, so they quit listening and went back to their marbles.

"There's no way they could do that! No way!" John Alan informed know-it-all Rachel Elizabeth Dalton, the bearer of this shocking Rose Bowl bulletin. Rachel's father was the editor of *The Apache*

Republican newspaper, and he had a Teletype machine, so she always thought she knew all the important news before anybody else. That was one reason John Alan didn't like her. There were lots more.

"There's no way they could move that great big stadium," Jimmy Johnson drawled. Jimmy talked so slow an ant could crawl from here to Oklahoma City before he finished. That's what John Alan told him anyway. "That place holds about ... about a hundred million people," Jimmy figured, scratching his scalp hard with both hands. (Teachers frequently checked Jim for head lice.) "A herd of elephants couldn't move somethin' that big!"

"They're not moving the stadium, ninny," Rachel retorted, smacking him on the top of his head. Then she remembered the lice. John Alan nearly busted a gut laughing when he saw her spit in her palm and rub it on her skirt before she added, "It's the football game they're moving!"

"But why'd they do a dumb thing like that?" John Alan demanded to know. "They've never done that in the whole history of football! I know about stuff like the Rose Bowl game!"

John Alan was sure he was the only kid in Apache, probably the only kid in Oklahoma, who had actually watched a Rose Bowl football game in person. Last January, he and his parents had driven two whole days from their home in California to watch Stanford, where his father went to college, beat Nebraska, his mother's alma mater, 21 to 13. It had been a great game, but he wasn't allowed to talk about it anymore. His father, who was the new superintendent of schools in this dinky little Podunk town, wouldn't let him talk about anything that happened before the two of them moved to Apache. Alone. Not even stuff like that trip to the Rose Bowl.

"W-e-l-l, this is one football fact you obviously don't know!" Rachel smirked. She sure was enjoying having his attention. She was going to drag this conversation out all day. "You see, John Alan ... the whole thing started right after Pearl Harbor got bombed. ..."

"Boys and girls! Boys and girls!" Miss Cathcart yelled as she ran in the room like a pack of hounds was about to tree her. Miss Cathcart had a hard time getting to school by 8:30 and an even harder time taking charge of her class once she got there. "Take your seats! Take your seats and get quiet right now!" she begged as she ripped off her cap and coat and threw them on the floor in the corner.

"We got a real important discussion going here," John Alan growled at her over his shoulder. "We'll sit down when we finish." He always talked to Miss Cathcart that way. He could get away with it, too, because she was nothing but a fraidy-cat, first-year teacher, and John Alan's father was her boss.

"Well ... well, I guess ... if it's really important ..." Miss Cathcart stammered. "You ... you may ... you may have one more minute!" Then she put her hands on her hips and tried to look taller. "But that's all you get, John Alan Feester, Jr.!" she threatened in a very thin voice. "We've got to get started on our lessons!"

"Finish the story, Rachel!" John Alan prodded. He was clear out of patience with her. "Where are they moving the Rose Bowl and why?"

"It's goin' to some town in North Carolina ... can't remember the name ... but I think it starts with a D." Her eyes got big, and with that red hair of hers she looked a lot like Little Orphan Annie. "It's being moved because the Japanese and Germans and Italians were all gonna sail their battleships right up to the beach in California and shoot cannonballs in the middle of the football field! They were gonna kill everybody at that game! All the players and the people in the stands, too! My father got the story right off his Teletype machine, and that Teletype machine ... unlike some *people* I know ... doesn't lie!"

4

"I'm pretty sure there's not a country in the world that still shoots cannonballs, Rachel," her best friend Paul told her, shaking his head back and forth. He slid in his seat and began to sketch a very big battleship that covered an entire sheet in his Big Chief tablet. Paul Griggs was a great artist. He was also the only kid in grade school who read the newspapers every day, so he knew almost as much as John Alan. Almost, but not quite.

"Well, everybody in the world knows the *Japanese* have lots and lots of battleships," Rachel replied. "I bet you know a bunch about Japanese battleships, don't you, John Alan?" She poked Paul on the arm and rolled her eyes when he looked up. Paul went back to his picture and ignored both the poke and the rolling eyes, but John Alan took note of them. He wondered what she was up to this time. Rachel was always up to something.

"I'm not believing they're moving that game till I hear it on the radio or read it in the newspaper," he told her, sauntering off to his seat. "I need a more reliable source than you! I know for a fact it's Oregon State versus Duke in the Rose Bowl this year, and Duke *is* in Durham, North Carolina," he rattled on like a walking, talking sports encyclopedia.

John Alan loved football. He was going to play

quarterback for Stanford someday, but he wasn't supposed to discuss Stanford either. There were so many things he was forbidden to talk about, it was hard for him to keep track. He'd found out that secrets have a way of chewing holes in the sack you stuff them in, and when he slipped up, he had to patch those holes with new lies real quick. Rachel had caught him in a few of them, but he was getting better at covering his tracks. The only trouble was, he'd lied so much it was getting harder for him to sort out the truth from the lies.

He saw that Rachel was still standing there with her hands on her hips, so he hollered back at her, "More than likely you're a prevaricator, Rachel. Besides that, we all know you're full of beans!"

"You belligerent enigma!" Rachel muttered loud enough for him to hear. She made a face and stalked over like she was going to smack him in the head, too. Just then Miss Cathcart walked up, tapped Rachel on the shoulder, and motioned for her to take her seat.

Until today, he didn't think this war had much to do with him, but if Rachel was right about the Rose Bowl, he might have to rethink the situation. When President Franklin D. Roosevelt went on the radio and announced that the United States of America was going to war, John Alan had to listen because Miss Cathcart brought a radio to school and put it right in the middle of her desk. She'd never brought a radio to school before, not even when the Yanks played the Dodgers in the World Series last October, and John Alan figured a World Series was more important than a World War.

Anyway, John Alan listened, and when the president's speech was over, he yelled and cheered like all the other kids in Theodore Roosevelt Elementary School because it was the patriotic thing to do. The president explained that America had to declare war because the Japanese had bombed the U.S. Navy base in Pearl Harbor. But John Alan had never even heard of that place. Why should he care about what happened somewhere in the middle of the Pacific Ocean?

The way he figured it, a ten-year-old kid who lived in a dinky town in Oklahoma didn't have to worry about a stupid war. Anybody who'd ever seen a map of the U.S.A. knew Oklahoma was smack dab in the middle of the forty-eight states. Now, a kid who lived in California or New Jersey might have something to worry about. Those states were right next to oceans. Enemy battleships could sail up, shoot their guns, and sail right off again. But Oklahoma? No battleship could get to Oklahoma. No way. Rachel was just trying to get his attention with all that war talk.

John Alan knew how to get Rachel's attention. Call her "Red." That turned her face the color of a Coke sign every time. She let her big brother, Al, call her that, but John Alan figured that was because Al's hair was as red as Rachel's. John Alan knew she liked her big brother a lot, and it seemed to him that Al was nicer to her than most brothers were to their kid sisters. Even though Al was a junior in high school, he didn't act like he minded Rachel hanging around him.

John Alan wished he had a brother. He wished he had red hair, too. Red or any other shade hair except brown like his mother's. His straight brown hair and dark brown eyes were exactly like his mother's. People back in California were always saying he looked like her. He used to like that, but he didn't want to look like her anymore.

His mother. She was the biggest subject he wasn't allowed to talk about, that mother of his. His father had told everybody in this crummy little town that his mother was dead, but that was a big fat lie, too.

John Alan liked making Rachel mad. He liked doing that almost as much as he liked football. In fact, the first time he laid eyes on her, the very first day of school, he made her so mad she declared war on him before they even ate their lunches.

John Alan, who had a head full of big words, called Rachel an oppugner that morning. He knew she'd have to get a dictionary for that one! He was sure he was the only kid in town who knew that an oppugner is a person who fights with words instead of weapons. John Alan let them all know then and there that he was the best oppugner in the fifth grade, maybe in the whole school.

Before that week was over, he found out Rachel had a big vocabulary, too—very big in fact, even if *oppugner* wasn't in it. She informed him that her family kept a dictionary in every single room of their house, even the kitchen, and her father made her learn at least one new word every single day. John Alan had to admit that, even though she was too big for her britches, she was pretty smart.

Paul called Rachel a "resister" because of the way she stood up to John Alan. But the way John Alan saw things, Rachel retreated a whole lot more than she resisted. Thinking about Rachel and plotting against her took John Alan's mind off his other problems. Some of the time anyway.

But that was all before Pearl Harbor got bombed and before he found out the Rose Bowl was being moved. Then he discovered something even more amazing. Rachel thought he was a spy for the Japanese and wanted to get him deported to another country!

When he found all those things out, he decided the war President Roosevelt declared on December 8 *did* have something to do with him after all.

CHAPTER 2
The Missing Mother

The way John Alan found out Rachel thought he was a spy was by spying on her. He knew she and Paul were up to something when they acted like such goody two-shoes that Miss Cathcart had to pick both of them for the W.O.W. on the same day. John Alan hated the W.O.W., which stood for "Words of Wisdom." The kid Miss Cathcart thought behaved best for the whole week got to pick a saying in her big *Bartlett's Familiar Quotations* book and write it in a fancy box on the blackboard. Sometimes two kids got to do it together. But never John Alan. Not once since he moved to this crummy town had he gotten to stay after school and decorate the blackboard with colored chalk. He'd been able to snooker Miss Cathcart into all sorts of other special favors, but not the W.O.W.

Even though he tried not to pay any attention to them, one of those Words of Wisdom sayings hit him right between the eyes. The one about secrets. "Three may keep a secret, if two of them are dead," Benjamin Franklin had said, and John Alan knew for sure those were wise words. That was why he never told any of his.

When he was sure Rachel and Paul were alone in the classroom to write their saying, he crouched down under the window next to the spot where all the kids played marbles. Then he did what he liked to do best: eavesdrop.

"What topic do we want?" That was Paul's voice.

"Something about spies or traitors, of course." That was Rachel.

"No, Rachel, we don't want to tip John Alan off." When he heard his name, he jerked off both earmuffs and moved his right ear closer to the window, even though it was colder than a well-digger's bottom out there. "John Alan's not as dumb as you wish he was," Paul was saying. "You say he's dumb because you don't like him. Actually, he's very smart."

John Alan smiled and rubbed his ears with his

gloved hands. Paul was the only kid in this Podunk town he liked. That was why, when he saw Paul steal Rachel's pencil box out of her desk that first day of school, he didn't tell. He just stuffed Paul's secret into his own secret sack and kept his mouth shut. Rachel, of course, thought he, John Alan Feester, Jr., had taken her dumb old pencil box. In fact, that pencil box was what had started this war between the two of them.

Hard as he tried, he couldn't figure out why Paul had stolen it. It did have all kinds of neat things in it—like a lid that slid out to become a ruler, a pair of pointed silver scissors, and dog-shaped erasers with eyes that moved. But Paul was Rachel's best friend, and stealing from her was a bad thing to do. John Alan did bad things himself sometimes, so he didn't waste a lot of time wondering about Paul and the pencil box. Yep, John Alan did bad things, too.

Especially after his mother left. Ran away, that is.

"Your mother did not 'leave' John Alan," his father had told him about a million times. "When a person *leaves,* they sometimes come back. Your mother ran off. Obviously, she ran away with another man. She ran away, and she's never coming back! That kind of behavior is not acceptable in a town like Apache, not for the wife of a candidate for school superintendent. That's why I had to tell the school board she was dead. Death is acceptable. Deserting your husband and child is not."

There was no way his father could know for sure that she would never come back, John Alan told himself often. Nobody could know that for sure. He didn't believe what his father said about that other man, either, since he'd never seen such a person.

John Alan loved his mother very much—so much that when he thought about her (and he thought about her every day) he often got so sick he wanted to throw up.

He did throw up sometimes. Once, back in California, he threw up all over his desk at school. That yucky puke even ran down the ink well and ruined his illustrated copy of *Wind in the Willows*. Even though it wasn't about football, *Wind in the Willows* was his all-time favorite book. His mother read it to him every night, even after he was too old for animal stories. Mr. Toad of Toad Hall was John Alan's favorite since Mr. Toad was always in trouble. When John Alan was little, his mother called him "Toad" when he was bad. When he thought about her now, he tried to remember to call her "Toad" instead of Mother, but sometimes he forgot.

That had been an awful day, the day he threw up

at school. The teacher and all the other kids thought it was because he had eaten too much. He did that a lot now—ate too much. So did his father. In fact, his father spent most of his time at home in the kitchen cooking all kinds of strange food. Eating kept them from having to talk to each other. Sometimes it even kept them from thinking. He liked the eating, but he missed the talking. And there was no way he could stop the thinking. About California. About his mother . . . about Toad.

He leaned closer to the cold bricks and tuned back in to Rachel and Paul. They were still discussing spies and traitors. Why were they so interested in spies and traitors? It must be because they listened to that stupid "Captain Midnight" on the radio all the time. That was all they talked about at recess. Captain Midnight said this about the war, Captain Midnight said that about the enemy. Who cared what a dumb, made-up radio character thought about the war anyway? According to the kids who listened to that program, there were spies, traitors, and saboteurs hiding behind every rock in Oklahoma. John Alan had more important things to worry about than spies, traitors, and saboteurs. Who did they think was a traitor anyway?

"At least look under treason," Rachel was saying.

Why would they put something like that in *Bartlett's* quote book? John Alan wondered as he tried to keep his feet from freezing by wiggling his toes around in his shoes. What famous person talked about treason and spies? No, wait a minute! Paul just said what he was reading came from the Constitution of the United States! Why was he reading something from the Constitution?

"Treason ... treason ... here it is! The very first one says 'Treason ... against ... the ... United ... States'!" Paul's voice sliced slowly through the cold December air like a dull knife.

"That's exactly what we're lookin' for!" Rachel shouted. "John Alan is a traitor who has committed treason!"

At the sound of his name again, John Alan had to clamp both hands over his mouth as fast as he could to keep from whooping out loud and giving away his hiding place.

He was the person Rachel thought was a traitor! What a joke! But she didn't sound like she was joking! This was great! Really great! The funniest thing that had happened to him since he moved to this stupid town! He was sure glad he had his gloves on. They helped muffle his guffaws.

"'Treason against the United States shall consist

only in levying war against them, or in adhering to their enemies, giving them aid and comfort,'" Paul read in a voice that sounded just like Edward R. Murrow on the radio.

"Aid and comfort to the enemy," Rachel repeated solemnly. "Wait! Keep on reading! Here's what we've been looking for. 'No person shall be convicted of treason unless on the testimony of two witnesses to the same overt act, or on confession in open court.' Hurrah! All it takes to convict somebody of treason is two witnesses! You and me! I was afraid it would take a lot more than that! John Alan Feester is deported already!"

John Alan doubled over, trying not to crow like a rooster who had just seen the sun. He could hear Rachel beating on something with her fists and was glad for the extra noise to help cover any sounds he might be making.

"Now all we have to do is spy on him until the two of us witness him doing something awful," she went on. "Something like signaling enemy aircraft at night with a flashlight or sneaking aboard an American ship with a bomb in a suitcase. We just have to be sure that both of us see him do it because it says we have to have two witnesses. You and me."

John Alan dropped to his hands and knees and

started crawling toward the end of the building. He had to get out of there before he lost control and gave himself away. The ground was cold and hard on his knees, but he didn't care. He'd heard enough to know what Rachel and Paul were up to.

"Aid and comfort to the enemy ..." He was pretty sure they were reading from Miss Cathcart's *Bartlett's Quotations,* but he needed to read that whole article in the Constitution about traitors. That wouldn't be hard to find. He'd go to the town library and look it up. If he was going to pretend to be a spy as well as a traitor, he wanted to know exactly what they did to those people if they got caught.

This war of Mr. Roosevelt's was going to be fun! Now he could spend all his time "spying for the enemy" overseas instead of worrying about the Toad in California.

CHAPTER 3
The Best-Laid Plans

John Alan spent all day Saturday thinking up ways to convince Rachel and Paul they were right about him being a spy. His father had a bunch of meetings, something about the new gym they were getting ready to build for the high school. Other than warning him not to discuss the past, John Alan's father pretty much let him do as he pleased. "Keep your nose clean," was the only advice he ever gave him. John Alan carried a big handkerchief and honked into it from time to time, especially at the dinner table, because it always made his father frown suspiciously.

His father's new job took up most of his time,

that and cleaning the house and cooking. He refused to hire help because they might snoop around and find out things, so he and John Alan had to do all the work. That took a lot of John Alan's time, but since he wasn't allowed to have friends over, it gave him something to do after school. Mr. John Alan Feester, Sr., didn't have much time left for John Alan Feester, Jr., or for thinking about the past either, the way John Alan saw things. Now this great war was going to keep John Alan from thinking about the past, too.

A spy! Rachel actually thought he was a spy! He could spend his days and nights thinking up traitorous things she and Paul could "witness."

First he tried to dye his yellow slicker black so he could sneak around at night like spies he'd seen in the movies. But the hot water he boiled it in melted the slicker into a great big sticky blob. He buried it in the back yard, metal pot and all, so his father wouldn't find it and ask questions. If the subject ever came up, he'd say he'd donated it to the Red Cross to send to the orphans in England. The Red Cross was always collecting for the orphans these days.

He'd heard enough of their conversation to know that Rachel and Paul were getting ready to go through his desk, so he spent the better part of an hour trying to remember if he had anything in there that could be considered evidence. He hoped so. If Rachel saw that picture of Gypsy Rose Lee with those fans, she'd be ready to call the police for sure. However, they didn't deport people for owning pictures of half-naked women. At recess he'd told the guys his father had taken him to a girly show at the State Fair, which wasn't true, of course, but it sure made their eyes bug out. He got asked to tell that story a bunch of times.

The truth was that the picture of Gypsy Rose Lee was a going-away present from Robby Barlow. Robby's big brother really *did* go to a girly show once, and he told John Alan and Robby that at the end of the show the woman only had on three Band-Aids! So John Alan stole that story and said that's what *he* had seen, a woman wearing three Band-Aids! John Alan found out that telling lies was kind of like drawing pictures, except you used words instead of crayons. He learned right away if he colored the story up a bunch, nobody paid much attention to details.

Thinking about that picture, which had come from the State Fair of California, reminded him he'd won five Hawaiian leis throwing a football through a tire at the state fair of Oklahoma. He'd taken two of those leis to school, and he couldn't find the other three anywhere, even though he tore the house apart looking for them. If he could find those leis, he'd hang them in his bedroom window. That would trick Rachel and Paul into thinking he brought them back from Hawaii! Then they could be the two witnesses needed to get him deported! It might be a start anyway, especially if he could find a hula skirt somewhere to put with the leis. Maybe he could even find a fresh pineapple to take in his lunch!

He dug up two flashlights and replaced the batteries so the beams would be real strong. He'd wait until after dark some night, lure Rachel and Paul out to the playground at school, and pretend he was signaling enemy aircraft. He'd figured out how to climb out his window without making a sound, and he even put oil on the boards in the floor of his room so they wouldn't squeak. He practiced opening and closing the bedroom window until he got too cold.

He looked up Rachel and Paul's phone numbers and wrote them down on a piece of paper and put it in his jacket pocket. He could disguise his voice and call them on the telephone with tips about what he was going to do next. He'd call from the drug store so the operator wouldn't know who he was.

Then he had one more idea. He traced a great big map of the Hawaiian Islands he'd found in a book in the library when he was checking on the Constitution.

He marked all the important spots with big red X's and rolled the map up to make a very suspicious-looking tube. He took the tube and walked up and down the streets of town all Sunday afternoon, waiting to be spotted and followed, but he didn't lay eyes on Rachel or Paul either one. That was strange. After all the things he'd heard them say when he was eavesdropping, he expected them to be hot on his trail.

It wasn't until Monday morning, when he ran into Jimmy on the playground, that he found out why Rachel and Paul had vanished from the streets for the entire weekend.

It wasn't John Alan who was going to be deported. It was Paul! Paul, the only kid in town John Alan liked, was moving! To make matters worse, he was moving to California! Hearing that made John Alan think about his mother ... Toad ... for the first time in three whole days.

He threw up his breakfast, but not where anybody could see him.

CHAPTER 4
Paul Gets Deported

John Alan felt a huge wave of jealousy slosh over him when Jimmy told him Paul's father had come home and was moving the Griggs family to California. Jimmy lived next door to Paul, so his mother had heard the details from Paul's mother on their way to church. John Alan and Jimmy huddled next to the building waiting for the bell to ring while Jimmy slowly strung his story on the story line. It was cold and blustery, so they had to pull the collars on their coats up near their ears and stomped their feet a lot.

"Paul's pa had been gone since before Halloween, ya know," Jimmy whispered as if a parent being gone a while was a big, dark, horrible secret. "Since before Halloween ... and here it is almost Christmas! My mother said she knew Mr. Griggs'd come home for Christmas. Ma said no father in his right mind would not come home for Christmas." He took two candy canes out of his pocket and began to suck on one, but he didn't offer John Alan the other one. He wouldn't have taken it, but Jimmy should have offered. "Yep, my ma knew old man Griggs would be back for Christmas!"

John Alan wanted to punch Jimmy in the stomach, smash him in the face, and ask him if all that stuff he was mouthing off about applied to mothers as well as fathers. He wanted to scream in Jimmy's face that his own mother had been gone eight months, three weeks, and four days, and Jimmy had better just shut his mouth about parents who went away and didn't come back for Christmas.

If his mother ... if Toad *did* come back to their old house, she wouldn't even be able to find them since they didn't live in that house anymore! They didn't even live in that state anymore! What would she do then? He wanted to shout these things at Jimmy.

But he didn't, of course. He wasn't allowed to do or say any of those things. He'd had so much practice acting like he felt one way when he really felt an-

25

other way, he was good at it now. Most of the time he could laugh when he wanted to cry without even having to work at it.

Since the day he got to this crummy town, he had acted like he was an awful person even though he really wasn't an awful person at all. He did it so nobody would ask him to come home with him, nobody would want to be his friend, and most of all, so nobody would ask him a bunch of questions.

Once in a while, though, he wasn't sure he hadn't become an awful person for real, and that worried him. But he didn't know what to do about it.

He took a deep breath and pushed the anger down through his body and into the ground. He was getting good at that, too, but it took a while, and Jimmy gave him a puzzled frown as they both stamped their feet up and down so they could feel their toes again.

Finally, John Alan sighed, "Get on with the story about the move, Jimmy! I know all about Mr. Griggs being a bum. You've told me about a hundred times, and it took a year every time you told it."

"Well, Paul's old man's got this cockamamie idea that him and Paul's mom can make about a billion dollars doin' war work in California, so they're moving there the end of the month! Paul don't want to, of course, but he ain't got no say. Kids never got no say, ya know." He bit the crook off the candy cane and began to crunch on it.

"Yeah, I know," John Alan sighed as he chewed the inside of his lip. "Kids never get any say." He had begged his father not to move, promised to be good the rest of his life if they could just stay right where they were. Right where she saw them last. But his father said they needed a fresh start in a place where nobody knew the truth about his mother. John Alan tried to kick a big rock that was half buried in the winter-packed dirt of the playground, but the rock wouldn't budge. He smashed down on it with the heel of his shoe and felt an instant stone bruise. He was glad. The hurt in his foot matched the one in his chest.

"Guess Rachel's one jump ahead of a fit," Jimmy drawled on when he'd dissolved the last of the candy cane. He clapped his hands together and blew on them. "They been best friends a hundred years. Nothin' she can do about it either, though." He took the second candy cane and began to rake it up and down the bricks.

"Who cares what Rachel thinks?" John Alan snarled, grabbing the candy cane out of Jimmy's hand and breaking it in two. Paul's moving changed everything, threw a great big wet blanket over all the fun he was planning to have. Paul and Rachel would be too busy worrying about the move to pay any attention to his great spy clues now.

It was a stupid idea anyway, he told himself as Jimmy shoved him into the wall and stalked off. Trying to convince them he was a spy and a traitor was a stupid idea, as stupid as Rachel thinking he'd had something to with Pearl Harbor. He might as well throw away the map, put the flashlights back where they belonged, and stop looking for leis and pineapples. Now all he had left to think about was California. And Toad. And whether or not he was really a bad person. He stomped the rock again.

There was one thing he could do. Before Paul left, he could let them know he had discovered their silly suspicions, and that he thought Rachel was the dumbest person who had ever been born. He wanted her to know he was laughing at her. Nobody likes to be laughed at. He was sure Paul had only gone along because they were best friends, but they both needed punishing now. And he was going to enjoy making Rachel squirm!

The bell rang, and he made his way toward the line that was forming to go inside the building, plotting his revenge with every step.

* * *

When he got home from school that afternoon, he got the notes he had taken at the library out of his desk. He'd copied the quote from the Constitution of the United States word for word, because he thought it might give him ideas. "Treason against the United States," it said, "shall consist only in levying war against them, or in adhering to their enemies, giving them aid and comfort."

Well, he couldn't levy any more war against Rachel than he already had. But since she was the enemy, he sure could have fun giving her "aid and comfort." All the "aid and comfort" she could take, in fact.

CHAPTER 5
Aiding Mr. Dalton

John Alan knew it wouldn't be hard to find Rachel and Paul together during the Christmas vacation. They'd been walking around like a couple of Siamese twins since they heard Paul was leaving, but the chance to give "aid and comfort" came sooner than he expected.

The first Saturday morning of Christmas vacation, his father asked him to drop the school board minutes off at Rachel's father's newspaper office. When he opened the door, there they were—staring down into Mr. Dalton's old Royal typewriter as if they were watching a pot that wouldn't boil.

Mr. Dalton explained he'd dropped a box of paperclips into the key well, and the three of them were having a hard time getting the last clip out. The typewriter wouldn't work until they did.

"I'll bet I have something to aid you," John Alan informed him, punching the word "aid" as if it were a doorbell that wouldn't ring. He then whipped out the Swiss army knife he'd gotten for his birthday. He narrowed his eyes at Rachel to be sure she was listening. She always paid close attention to what he said to be certain she knew the meaning of every word. John Alan was sure he'd never said he would "aid" anybody and neither had Rachel.

She noticed the new word. He could tell by the look on her face.

He smirked at her and, when Mr. Dalton looked away for a moment, he acted as if he was about to do something really sneaky—something like dump a bottle of ink into the key well or push the typewriter off the table.

He waited for Rachel to react. It didn't take long.

"Don't you touch my daddy's typewriter!" she hollered. "Don't you dare lay a finger on it, you saboteur, you! You and that Benedict Arnold Johnson spy friend of yours. Go back to the Flying Red Horse where you belong!"

John Alan had no idea what she meant about Mr.

Johnson and the Flying Red Horse filling station, but he did know what she meant when she called him a saboteur. Stupid "Captain Midnight" fans talked about "spies, traitors, and saboteurs" all the time. Her calling him a saboteur was as much fun as being called a spy or traitor. He slapped an amazed and puzzled look on his face and sighed a big sigh as he shrugged his shoulders at her father.

"Rachel, what has gotten into you?" Mr. Dalton asked in a very irritated tone of voice. "John Alan is just trying to be helpful, and I, for one, appreciate it."

John Alan shook his head sadly and made his face a complete blank as he searched for the correct section of his knife. He opened it up, used the tweezer-like blade to remove the paperclip, and flipped the clip to Mr. Dalton. Then he strolled out the front door without saying a word.

The seed of suspicion had been planted. He could see that Rachel and Paul knew he was up to something, but they had no idea what it was. Not yet.

But the day wasn't over, and John Alan, who needed the two of them to stay together, was about to get lucky again.

CHAPTER 6
Solving the Enigma

John Alan spied them before he got to the front door of Carter's Drug Store that afternoon, so he was ready with all the right words. He'd been rehearsing what he was going to say since he left the newspaper office that morning. Rachel and Paul were coming into Carter's just as he was going out.

"Well," he burst out in a jovial, Merry-Christmas tone, "we meet again! You two wouldn't be following me, would you? Are you in need of more *aid* and *comfort?* I am so glad I was able to aid your father, Rachel. When you need *aid,* just call on me. I gladly give *aid* ... and *comfort,* too, any time I have the opportunity." He almost doubled over laughing, but he managed to get out the door without dropping any of the packages he was carrying. He stood outside and mouthed the words "aid and comfort" several times before he left.

There! He had done it! He knew it wouldn't take them long to figure out why he kept saying "aid and comfort" over and over again. Rachel would remember those words came from the Constitution, since she had been so excited about finding them. Then Paul would remind her where they were when they read about "aid and comfort to the enemy." Room 5B of Theodore Roosevelt Elementary School. Where Miss Cathcart's windows were always open! He was positive that Paul, who read Sherlock Holmes all the time, would be able to deduce that he had eavesdropped on their conversation and knew they thought he was a spy! But just to double check, he needed to watch a little bit longer.

He got way over in the corner of the front window of Carter's so he could see without being seen. He watched them slide into a booth across from each other and give Miss Cathcart's sister their order. When she left, he could tell they were talking about what happened when they came in because Rachel kept pointing toward the front door. Before long, he saw Paul slap his hands on the table. He could tell by the defeated look that began to spread over Rachel's face that Paul was telling her what he had just deducted, that John Alan was a sneaky eavesdropper who had heard every word they said that day. He had heard them say they thought he was a spy!

Now Rachel knew why he'd been laughing so hard when he left them at the front door. She knew he thought she was a dumb twerp, and that he'd be offering her "aid and comfort" every time he saw her for the rest of her life. She looked miserable, and he was glad.

John Alan smiled and started to turn away when he saw Rachel's brother and a soldier he didn't recognize come up and sit down in their booth. The soldier punched Paul on the shoulder and mussed his hair. He gave Rachel a great big grin, and Rachel beamed back at him. It sure didn't take her very long to forget him and his "aid and comfort" threat.

He decided to watch a little longer. He looked from one smiling face in that booth to another, and as he did, he found himself wishing that he was sitting in there at that table with them ... with Rachel's big brother and that soldier. Even with Rachel and Paul.

That could never happen, of course. Even if they knew he was outside watching them, wishing he had friends like them, they'd never ask him to join them now. Why should they? He'd ruined any chance for friendship when he let Rachel know he was never going to stop "aiding and comforting" her. He wished he could stop watching and go on home, but he couldn't.

Miss Cathcart's sister delivered a great big tray of food to their table. She smiled as she plopped down baskets of burgers and fries in front of each of them and lifted four large glasses of Coke from her tray. She smiled again when the soldier drained his Coke in one gulp and handed it back to her for a refill. She wiggled her way back to the soda fountain while all the boys, John Alan included, watched her go.

She was wiggling her way back through the crowd with the refill when the soldier in Rachel's booth spied a marine who had just walked in the door. The soldier jumped up and pretended to have a football in his hand. He pulled his arm back for a pass, and the marine jumped high in the air to make the imaginary catch. In the process, the marine knocked the tray, Coke and all, through the air and into the lap of Mr. White, the pharmacist, who was seated in his wheelchair at the end of counter. Mr. White sat there with that Coke running down his face and glasses and laughed as if it was the funniest thing that had ever happened to him while everybody in the drug store cheered as if their team had just won the championship.

Suddenly, John Alan was very cold.

And very hungry.

And very sad.

He turned away from the window and trudged home.

CHAPTER 7
Prince Albert
in a Can

The last week of December was a miserable time for most of the world, John Alan included. His father spent almost all of the time cooking and trying to get John Alan to eat, but everything he chewed stuck in his throat. And when he did finally manage to swallow, it lumped into a big hard ball in his stomach. He took the orange and apple out of his Christmas stocking, but he didn't even bother with the candy.

He got lots of presents: a train set with a town and trees and bridges; a Mr. Marvelous magic set;

five sports books, a baseball and bat from one grand-mother; and four sports books and a football from the other grandmother. The magic set had "For Children 4-8" plainly marked on the top of the box. He already had two footballs, he'd read all the sports books but one, and the train broke the day after Christmas. They had to mail it off to get it fixed.

There had also been a gift from his mother.

It had been mailed to their old house in California early in December, but since it had to be forwarded to Apache, it didn't arrive until New Year's Eve. He was alone when he received it at the post office.

When they first moved to town, it had taken John Alan a week to remember to pick up the mail every day. Where he lived in California, a mailman delivered right to his house. Here he had to pick everything up at the post office because mailmen only delivered in the country, and his father often couldn't get downtown until after the window closed.

When John Alan saw the little green package notice through the glass window in their box, his heart began to pound very hard. He had been hoping for a present from her since Thanksgiving. The package notice was the only thing in their box. His fingers were trembling so bad, he had to work the box combination three times before he got it to open. He looked around to see if anybody was watching him, but they were all busy getting their own mail. He grabbed the slip, slammed the box shut, and stared at the little green rectangle for almost a full minute. It had his name on it. He finally marched to the counter and presented the paper to Mr. Kizer, the postmaster.

"Well, hello there, Mr. Feester, Jr.!" Mr. Kizer boomed. John Alan wished the man hadn't shouted his name out like that. Now everybody in town knew he had gotten a package. "And a Happy New Year to you! Looks like somebody's getting a late Christmas present!" He reached under the counter and produced a cigar-box-sized package. "Haven't taken up smoking cigars, have you?" Mr. Kizer teased as he handed the package to John Alan, who muttered a quick "No!" and rushed out the door.

The package was addressed to "Mr. John Alan Feester, Jr.," in his mother's beautiful, flowing calligraphy. The "Jr." was done in bright red ink, but the rest of the words were in black. There was no return address. The postmark read "Los Angeles."

He put the package in his bike basket and pedaled home as fast as he could go without the box bouncing out. He was relieved to find that his father wasn't home yet. Running straight into the house, he didn't even take off his coat before he opened the box. He carefully peeled the brown outer wrapping off to save the handwriting. The present inside was wrapped in silver paper, but there wasn't any bow. A bow would have gotten smashed, he told himself as he loosened and removed the silver paper, and it would have taken her more time to wrap it, too. Maybe she was busy. He stared down into the box.

Inside was a statue of a silver angel with gold wings. It was wearing a football uniform with an "S" for Stanford on the front of the jersey. Instead of a harp, the angel was holding a gold football. The football was in the palm of the left hand (John Alan himself was a lefty) and the arm was cocked back as if a long pass was about to be attempted.

When he lifted the angel out of the box, he found a card under it. Actually, it was a sheet of plain old typing paper folded in two. The top half had his initials, J.A.F., in the same writing and red ink as was on the address. On the inside it said, "I had this made especially for you in the city named for the angels. I have asked her to watch over you. Believe it or not, I love you very much." There was no signature.

"I have asked *her* to watch over you," he read aloud. This dumb angel was a girl! You couldn't tell by looking since she had a football helmet on. Everybody knew there were no girl football players, at least no girl football players who wore uniforms. There sure weren't any girls who played for Stanford!

He shook his head as he put the angel back in the box and laid the piece of typing paper on top of her. He folded both the brown and silver wrappings until they were small enough to fit in the box also. Then he took the box into his room and hid it underneath an empty Buster Brown shoebox at the back of his closet. He'd kept that box because of the picture on top. He traced the frame around Buster Brown's dog, Tige, with his finger and wished for the one-hundredth time that he had a dog.

As he closed the closet door, he wondered if the angel was able to get that pass off without being sacked. He doubted it, since she was a girl. He started to open the box and check, but then he changed his mind and went downstairs. He decided not to tell his father.

***

The next morning John Alan got up early, checked to see if the box with the angel in it was still where he put it, and then went for a ride on his bike. His father was still asleep when he left. He'd done a lot of sleeping since the Christmas vacation started.

John Alan was pedaling down the street which ran in front of the school when he saw the same soldier who had been in the drug store with Rachel and Paul coming out of the Snows' house carrying an army duffel bag. Mr. Snow was the school janitor. He'd always been nice to John Alan, but John Alan figured that was because his father was Mr. Snow's boss. His father had told him the four Snow brothers lived with their grandparents because their parents had been killed in a car wreck. At least that's what everybody thought. John Alan knew for a fact that sometimes people said people were dead when they weren't.

There was a big crowd around the soldier, and when John Alan saw Miss Mae Ella Cathcart among them, he decided to do some more spying. They were so busy talking and taking pictures, they didn't notice John Alan parking his bike and sneaking along the outside of the fence that surrounded the garden, which was next to the house.

Mrs. Snow's garden was dead and brown now, but it had been filled with flowers when John Alan first moved to town. He liked to ride his bike back and forth by the fence and smell them. His mother ... Toad ... had grown flowers, too, and the fragrance of roses and honeysuckle reminded him of her and the fun they used to have reading in her garden. He wondered if she had a garden now. In Los Angeles, you could grow flowers all year long if you wanted to.

He crept closer to the fence. There was a little hole, so he could see as well as hear who was doing the talking. He recognized Mr. and Mrs. Snow and Rachel's brother, Al, along with the three Snow grandsons, so he guessed the soldier must be the oldest brother, the one who had joined the army last year. John Alan couldn't remember his name.

Ever since Pearl Harbor was bombed, the kids at school talked a lot about the Apache boys in the military. Miss Peevehouse, the librarian, fixed a big bulletin board next to the trophy case with a banner across the top that read "They Proudly Serve." Every time somebody new enlisted or was drafted, she got their picture and thumb-tacked it to the red, white, and blue construction paper background. He'd have to pay more attention to those pictures, John Alan decided as he watched the way everybody was patting and hugging that soldier. Miss Cathcart's sister had done that at the drug store, too.

"Hey, Gram, what you hiding there?" the soldier teased Mrs. Snow, who was holding her coat real tight to her body. "Must be a going away present for

me in that pocket! Bet it's gloves, isn't it? You tried
to give me gloves last time I left! Didn't need 'em in
Texas, but bet I will this trip!" He covered his mouth
with his hands like that monkey in the speak-no-evil
cartoons. John Alan was glad he wasn't a real spy because he was pretty sure Joe Bob had just said something he wasn't supposed to tell. "Loose lips sink
ships!" the navy poster in the library warned.

Mrs. Snow slid a Prince Albert tobacco can out of
the pocket of her black winter coat. "Now, don't you
laugh at this, Joe Bob Snow!" she warned him.
"Don't you laugh, or I'll take you out to the woodshed. You may belong to Uncle Sam now, but back
here you'll never be too old for a trip to the woodshed!" She held the can out with both hands but
looked down at the ground instead of at him.

"I'm not even gonna grin," the soldier assured
her, covering his mouth again as he accepted the can
from her. "Prince Albert in a can?" he crowed. "I
can't believe it! It was the woodshed for sure if you
caught us pullin' the old Prince Albert trick on Mr.
Carter at the drug store! Remember, Jack? You did it
best!"

"Ring, ring!" Jack responded, circling his hand
in the air as if he were cranking the handle of the
telephone. "Carter's Drug Store?" he inquired,

crackling his voice in imitation of an old man as he pretended to hold the receiver to his ear and talk into the mouthpiece. "It is? Well ... you got Prince Albert in a can? You do? Well, better let him out before he smothers!"

Miss Cathcart, who had been snapping Jack's picture as he talked, doubled over laughing—and so did all the other people huddled together out there in that cold, brown garden. That old Prince Albert joke wasn't very funny, but those people were sure laughing like it was.

"Want to explain yourself, Gram?" the soldier asked, giving her a hug. "Can't believe you're promoting the use of tobacco!"

They all turned to Mrs. Snow, but she was still staring down at the ground as if she were trying to count the leaves that were swirling around her scuffed, brown shoes. Mr. Snow patted her on the shoulder and cleared his throat before he spoke.

"Well, ya see, Joe Bob, your Gram's got it in her head you need some Oklahoma dirt to take along with you. You know her and this here dirt!" He pointed at the dead, dry flowerbeds. "Rather be digging her fingers in there than eat. That's a fact!" He cleared his throat again, and John Alan felt his own throat get tight. "That can ain't got tobacco in it,"

Mr. Snow went on, getting faster with every word. "It's full of dirt ... dirt from this here garden. She reckoned when you got lonesome you could sprinkle some of this dirt between your toes and wiggle 'em in some good old Oklahoma soil!" When he stopped talking, the only sound in the garden was the rustling of the leaves.

John Alan bit his lip and wished he hadn't stopped to eavesdrop. He had enough on his mind without having to worry about some guy he never even met going off to the war carrying a can of his grandma's dirt in his pocket!

"Now for the last picture," he heard the soldier call to Miss Cathcart. "I want Gram and Granddad sittin' in the swing with him singin' her her song! Y'all go do that so Mae Ella here can snap you. Hustle! It's almost bus time!"

They shuffled over to the swing and sat down. Mr. Snow pulled the old woman close to him and began to sing a song John Alan had never heard. It was about a flowing river not waking up sweet Mary, and by the way she smiled, John Alan decided Mary had to be Mrs. Snow's name.

"Say 'Kick the Krauts!'" Miss Cathcart hollered, and then she snapped. The old man and woman started to get up.

"No! Stay right there!" the soldier commanded them. "I ... I don't want you to come down to that old cold bus station to wave me away. I ... well ... every time I sprinkle that dirt between my toes, I want to see you sitting there. In that swing. And before you know it, you're going to look out the window, and I'll be sitting there myself again. Just sitting there, waiting for you to notice I've come home!" He ran over and gave them each a quick hug and then grabbed up his duffel bag.

There was another moment of silence before the brother named Jack yelled, "Hip-hip hooray for Gram's dirt! Let's hear it for the greatest quarterback of all time and his Prince Albert can!" Everybody began to laugh again and yell "Hip-hip hooray!" as John Alan scooted back down the fence and then began to run for his bicycle. He could still hear them cheering as he turned the corner toward home.

***

On New Year's Day, John Alan and his father listened to the Rose Bowl, which, as Rachel had informed him, had been moved from Pasadena, California, to Durham, North Carolina, because of the war. Oregon State slipped by Duke, 20 to 16, but John Alan didn't care much one way or another. He didn't know anybody who'd ever gone to either of those schools, and somehow football didn't seem as important since he'd watched those people tell that soldier good-bye.

He hoped when school started, he could get back to tormenting Rachel so he wouldn't have to think about all the other stuff that was happening all around him. That other stuff was really beginning to crowd up his head.

CHAPTER 8
The New Miss Cathcart

"My mama's the reporter for the Civil Defense League," John Alan could hear Rachel prattling as he plodded his way down the hall to 5B the first Monday in January. It was so cold he had ridden to school with his father in their big warm Buick, which was nice, but it put him at school very early. But not earlier than Rachel. "They're gonna wrap bandages and knit socks at the meeting today! Their motto is 'Lots to do in '42!' Can I put that on the blackboard? Please! Pretty please with sugar on it?"

John Alan paused outside the door to let her finish her stupid story. He didn't really want to eavesdrop on what she had to say this time, but Rachel's seat was right next to the door and he couldn't help hearing what she and Miss Cathcart were talking about.

"Go right ahead," he heard Miss Cathcart tell her. "But remember our 'pretty pleases' ... and everything else for that matter ... are going to have to do without sugar for The Duration. We'd all better start getting used to that," she told Rachel with a big sigh.

The Duration. He kept hearing grown-ups say those two words all the time—The Duration. He needed to find out what that meant. Evidently, Rachel knew, since she didn't ask. She always asked if she didn't know.

"Since Daddy owns the newspaper," Rachel babbled on, "Mama's the reporter for every club she's in. She says that's fine with her because she doesn't want to be president of anything. Presidents have to stand up and say things like, 'The meeting will now come to order.' Mama says having to do that in front of a whole bunch of people would make her break out in hives! I don't think I'd break out in hives if I was the president!"

That was just the cue John Alan needed to go in. The first day of school, when he started trying to keep anybody from liking him, he had bullied Miss Cathcart into making him class president so he could boss everybody around. If he wanted to keep the battle with Rachel going, he needed to hang on to that job.

"But you're *not* the president, are you, Rachel?" he announced as he swaggered in the door. "I am! So you don't have to worry about getting hives!" His eyes fell on Paul's empty desk. He could deliver her a double whammy. "I'm gonna switch seats," he informed Miss Cathcart. "Paul won't be needing this spot anymore!"

He wanted to let them know right away that it might be a new year, but he was still the same old John Alan Feester. If he let this world war soften him up, they might figure out how miserable he really was. He wanted Rachel to know their war was still on, too, Paul or no Paul. Taking his desk was a good way to start. He'd wait to remind her of "aid and comfort" at recess.

"Now, John Alan," Miss Cathcart began, but the bell interrupted her.

The room was quickly filled with screaming, yelling fifth graders who, as usual, were shoving each other around and throwing things.

Miss Cathcart pulled an enormous paddle they had never seen before out from under her desk and smacked it very hard on her hand. In a loud voice which could easily be heard above the din, she commanded: "Sit down and get quiet immediately!" She smacked her already red palm a second time with the paddle.

She'd never done anything like that before, never talked like that, never looked like that. The whole class, John Alan included, sat down and put their hands in their laps.

"Move back to your regular seat, John Alan Feester," she said, narrowing her eyes and pointing the paddle straight at him. "Move right this minute!"

John Alan started to say something, but then he changed his mind. He hadn't had time to move his books to Paul's desk, so he just got up, stomped back to his old desk, and flopped down. He frowned at Miss Cathcart, but she didn't seem to care.

"Ladies and gentlemen," Miss Cathcart began, and they all looked around to be sure she was talking to them. She always called them boys and girls before. "Today is not only the beginning of a new year, but also the beginning of a new way of life in America ... and in this classroom."

Nobody made a sound.

"Each of you is aware of the many changes going on across our great nation, changes which are going to affect all of us for quite some time." She looked slowly around the room, making eye contact with each student in the room. They had never seen her so serious and determined. She didn't look anything like the Miss Cathcart who had allowed John Alan to boss her around all the time.

"What ... what if we don't wanna change?" Agnes Ann challenged her. Next to John Alan, Agnes Ann was the nerviest kid in the class. "What if we like things the way they are? I wouldn't mind getting rid of my bratty little brother, but other than that, what I'd really like is for things to be like they were before December 7. I'm sick and tired of this old war anyway. That's all everybody talked about the whole Christmas vacation ... war, war, war! I didn't even get but one candy cane in my stocking this year! I'm sick of this war!" She crossed her arms and got a big frown on her face.

The class, John Alan included, turned to see how Miss Cathcart was going to answer that.

"Listen to me very carefully, Agnes Ann Billingsly! That kind of attitude will not be tolerated in this class- room. One candy cane, indeed! We have a great deal more to worry about than candy canes! We are Americans, and our freedom and the freedom of the civilized world is at stake here. We have no choice, no choice at all." Agnes Ann slid way down in her seat.

"Nobody *wanted* to go to war," Miss Cathcart admitted, her tone a little softer now, "but the choice was taken away from America when the enemy bombed our ships and killed our people. We had to declare war on the Axis Powers: Japan, Germany, and Italy, the countries who want to take freedom away from the whole world." She stopped talking and picked up a copy of *The Apache Republican*. John Alan saw Rachel break into a big grin.

"As you all know, Rachel's father is the editor of our town newspaper. Mr. Dalton, like most Americans, is a great admirer of the British prime minister, Winston Churchill," she went on as she folded the paper in half. "Last week, Mr. Dalton reprinted something Mr. Churchill said in June of 1940, long before the United States ... before we ... each of us in this room ... entered the war." She paused to scan the rows again. "What Mr. Churchill said to the people of England *then* will explain to you what is ahead of us in America *now*." She cleared her throat and began to read.

"...whatever the cost may be, we shall fight on the beaches, we shall fight on the landing ground, we shall fight in the fields and in the streets ..." She looked up to be sure she had the full attention of every student.

She did.

"We shall fight in the hills; we shall never surrender!" she finished as she slapped the paper back down on her desk with a loud pop. She looked at it a moment, and then back up at the class. "We are lucky that, so far, none of this horrible war is being fought on American soil. That may not be true in the future." She paused for a moment. "I want you to imagine how you would feel if the war was being fought right here in the United States of America, right here on our soil."

No one said a word. John Alan thought about that can of dirt Mrs. Snow gave Joe Bob—the Oklahoma soil he was going to sprinkle between his toes when he was in a foxhole overseas. Joe Bob might not even need that can of dirt to be fighting on the soil in Mrs. Snow's garden! Miss Cathcart was right! This war could come to America if our army couldn't win the war overseas.

"This V for victory has become Mr. Churchill's trademark," Miss Cathcart told them lifting her right hand up with her thumb holding the pinky and the ring fingers down to let the other two make a V. "Let's let it become ours, too."

John Alan was the first one to flash the V for victory back to her, but in seconds everybody else had his or her hand in the air, too. The day the president declared war, everybody had cheered and clapped, but nobody cheered and clapped now. They were all very, very quiet.

Miss Cathcart turned around and printed "Cents for Defense" on the blackboard, taking up almost all the space there was. She used a different piece of chalk for each letter in each word; red first, then white, then blue. It took her a whole two minutes, but no one in the room moved or made a single sound.

"Every Monday, each of you who has been able to save ten cents will get to march to the bank and buy a war stamp after roll has been taken," she told them. In one hand she held up a little red, white, and blue book that was about the size of a postcard. In the other she held a tiny piece of paper that looked like a miniature postage stamp. "You'll lick the stamp and stick it in the book. The first person to fill a book will get to wear this gold star for a week." She held up a big cardboard star with a V in the center of it. "Instead of buying candy bars or popcorn when you go to the picture show, you will want to save your money to buy war stamps."

"My daddy says there aren't going to be any candy bars to buy anyways," Jean Margaret piped up. "He says we're gonna send all the candy to the soldiers and sailors and marines so they'll have more energy to fight!"

"That's true, Jean Margaret," Miss Cathcart agreed. "They certainly are going to need a lot of energy, those military men."

She got a faraway look in her eyes, and John Alan figured she was thinking about Joe Bob Snow again. She sure had been hanging on to his hand and patting him on the shoulder a lot that day in Mrs. Snow's garden. Miss Cathcart and Joe Bob Snow! Every time he remembered that, he was surprised again. He didn't think teachers did things like hold hands, but evidently the war changed teachers, too. The war had sure made her tough all of a sudden.

The war was changing him, too, but he couldn't let other people know that. He took a deep breath, then blurted out, "What about our energy? We gotta have energy to walk clear down to the bank and back, don't we? I'm not giving up my candy bars for any old defense stamps!"

He hadn't even raised his hand, and after her reaction to Agnes Ann's whining, he knew Miss Cathcart wasn't going to like what he said.

"John ... Alan ... Feester, you should be ashamed of yourself!" she said, leaving big pauses between every word in his name. "The bank is only three blocks from here. It is certainly not going to wear you out to walk three blocks! Loyal American citizens will not complain!"

Out of the corner of his eye, he could see Rachel smirking at him.

Miss Cathcart jerked open her desk drawer, put the "Cents for Defense" book and stamp inside, and slammed it shut, glaring at him the whole time. He dropped his head and decided he'd gone too far. He'd better just stick to giving Rachel "aid and comfort" and leave this new Miss Cathcart alone.

CHAPTER 9
The Birth of Simon Green

"Now, ladies and gentlemen, as you know, the war is causing many people to change their occupations," Miss Cathcart began lecturing again. She had a smile on her face that looked as if it wanted to be somewhere else. John Alan could tell she was still mad at him, and he was sorry about that because he was starting to like the new Miss Cathcart. "Yes, many people are changing jobs, but your job remains the same. You are students and your job is to learn. Our first lesson on the first day of this new year will focus on calendars."

She walked to the wall next to the blackboard and took down the calendar that still had December across the top, but not before she traced the number seven with her finger. "A date that will live in infamy," she reminded the class. "You must never forget that date, ladies and gentlemen. Never."

She then unrolled a much larger calendar than the one she had taken down. This one had a picture of Uncle Sam pointing his finger and saying "I want you!" on it.

"We learn a lot from calendars. We look at this page, and what do we learn? We learn that today is January 5, 1942, a Monday."

"Next thing you know, she'll be teaching us to tell time," Jimmy whispered to John Alan. "What's she think we are, a bunch of baby first graders?"

"I heard that, Jimmy Johnson!" Miss Cathcart said, giving him the same cold glare she had given John Alan. "Kindly address any remarks about today's lesson to me rather than to John Alan Feester. I believe there is a great deal about calendars you don't know."

John Alan frowned at Jimmy and gave him the evil eye. She wasn't going to let people get away with acting bad, this new Miss Cathcart. The old fraidy-cat one had made it easy. Maybe she could even teach *him* to be good again. If he ever decided he wanted to be.

"Have any of you ever heard of or seen a perpetual calendar?" she asked.

Rachel was the only one who raised her hand.

"Well, Rachel, good for you! What can you tell us about perpetual calendars? First of all, what does *perpetual* mean? As big as your vocabulary is, I'm sure that word is in it."

"Perpetual: lasting for eternity; never ending," Rachel replied just like she was reading right out of a dictionary. John Alan bit his tongue to keep from whispering "aid and comfort! . . . aid and comfort!" to her. This new Miss Cathcart had better hearing than the old one. Either that or the class was quieter now. He wasn't sure which.

"That's correct, Rachel. And have you ever seen a perpetual calendar?"

"I have one! It's on the back of the closet door in my room," Rachel declared. "My aunt Lavern gave it to me for my fifth birthday."

John Alan couldn't stand it another minute. He rolled his eyes and raised his hand. Since this was the first time he had ever asked permission to speak, Miss Cathcart smiled and nodded at him.

"Bet she's making that up! Why would somebody

give a calendar to a five-year-old kid? What kind of dumb present is that?" he blurted out before he remembered the silver angel. He was sure glad Rachel didn't know about the angel. She was a pretty dumb present, too.

"I'll let Rachel answer that, John Alan, and hereafter please confine yourself to questions, not opinions."

John Alan slumped back in his desk.

"Because I was born on her birthday, the thirteenth of March, which was a Friday that particular year," Rachel prattled on. "It happened again the year I was five, another Friday the thirteenth! She taught me how to look up every birthday of mine ever so I'd know which ones will be on a Friday. Daddy said those Friday the thirteenth birthdays might bring us bad luck, but Aunt Lavern told him he must have triskaidekaphobia if he thought that!"

She stared straight at John Alan as she pronounced what had to be the largest word in her vocabulary, but he gave her a bored look to let her know he was not at all impressed.

"Triskaidekaphobia means a fear of the number thirteen," she added after a short pause.

"It does, indeed," Miss Cathcart smiled broadly. "And you were born in 1931, right? One of those rare years when there were three Friday the thirteenths! This year is another of those years, and that's what today's lesson is about." She lifted the pages on the big wall calendar to February, March, and November, pointing to the Friday the thirteenth on each sheet.

John Alan's hand shot up again. "Is that a real word?" he asked, since she'd warned him to only ask questions.

"Yes, triskaidekaphobia is a real word," she assured him as she turned to write it on the blackboard under *Cents for Defense*. She spaced it out, "tris-kai-dek-o-pho-bi-a," to show how it was pronounced. John Alan copied it down and immediately started to memorize the spelling.

"Does anyone else in the class have a birthday on the thirteen of any month?" Miss Cathcart asked, and Shirley Jean began to wave her arm back and forth like a train conductor signaling the engineer to go.

"Me! Me! Mine's in October, Miss Cathcart!"

"Shirley Jean—October 13," Miss Cathcart repeated as she wrote. "Anybody else?"

Rachel spoke out again. "Paul's is February 13, Miss Cathcart. I know he's not in our class anymore, but I ... I ... thought you'd like to know."

She stopped to look over at Paul's empty desk before she went on. "Since February has twenty-eight days this year, both of our birthdays are on Fridays this time. We were ... we were ..." She stopped and swallowed real hard. "We planned to have some kind of really big celebration, but then he had to move ..." Her voice trailed off, and for the first time ever, John Alan almost felt sorry for her.

"What a coincidence," Miss Cathcart said in a soothing tone. "You all being such good friends." She chalked *Paul—February 13* on the board above Shirley Jean's name and then put Rachel's name in between. "Our class will have to make Paul a birthday banner! We'll make it an art class project. I have a nice mailing tube I've been saving for just such an occasion! Let us know when you get an address."

Then she reached under her big desk, pulled out a brown grocery sack, and sat it on top. "Now, class, I have a little present for you from Mr. Schwartz at the meat market. Every year he gives almanacs to his customers, and this year he was kind enough to let me have a copy for each of you." She pulled out a handful of booklets and began to pass them out. "Open to page 204, 205, and 206."

"Jeepers creepers!" Billy Joe said with a whistle. "What a lotta numbers!"

The three pages contained a perpetual calendar. In a box at the top of the left side were all the years from 1775 through 2050 and after each year was a number. Then there were fourteen calendars with numbers that corresponded with the numbers by the years. On the first one, January 1 was on a Sunday, and that date moved through the days of the week as it went across the page to the next calendar. When a leap year came, as it does every four years, the date skipped a day.

"Two thousand fifty!" Agnes Ann said, looking at the last year listed. "We'll all be dead by then!"

"We'll all die of boredom by the time we finish this stupid lesson," Stanley added as he yawned, closed his eyes, scrunched down in his desk like he was taking a nap, and began to snore real loud.

"Stanley Wright, sit up and pay attention!" Miss Cathcart commanded, slapping the paddle on the desk again and then brandishing it at him as if it were a sword. He sat up and paid attention. John Alan gave Stanley a frown and the evil eye, too, but he didn't think Miss Cathcart noticed.

"Now, we are going to do a calendar drill," she said, sitting down on the corner of her desk and looking around the room. "I need a volunteer."

Every kid in the class shot their hands in the air and began to shout, "Me! Me! Pick me!" Every kid, that is, except Simon Green.

Simon had never raised his hand since he walked into the class in early December. He never even asked to go to the bathroom. He never said anything but "yes," "no," and "present." He had moved from another state, but nobody except Miss Cathcart, who had received his report card (straight A's in everything including attendance and deportment), knew the state was Pennsylvania. At first she had tried to get him to do or say something, but then Pearl Harbor came along, and she forgot about him. He was so quiet it was easy to forget he was in the room, but her eyes fell on him now.

"Simon, why don't we start with you?"

Simon looked down at his desk and didn't reply. Everybody else got real quiet because they wanted to hear Simon's voice. He never talked. Not ever. He hadn't even said anything at recess when John Alan called him "Simple Simon" and asked him if he'd ever met a pie man the day he joined their class. Simon had just looked down at the ground, kicked a rock, and walked away.

"Come on, Simon," Miss Cathcart said gently, "all you have to do is tell us when your birthday is. That's easy enough, isn't it? Then we'll see who can be the first to find out what day of the week you were born on and what day of the week it will be when you have your one hundredth birthday party! That's the kind of fun thing you can do with a perpetual calendar!"

There was a long period of silence.

"Simon," she repeated with just a hint of anger in her voice, "when's your birthday?"

"I don't know," Simon replied. It came out in a very soft whisper, but everybody in the class heard it. Simon Green had said, "I don't know."

More silence followed. Jimmy and Stanley looked at John Alan. So did a lot of other kids. He knew they were expecting him to prod an answer out of Simon, so he decided to do it.

"Aw, Simon, you're full of baloney! You're just afraid she's gonna write your birthday down in her planning book and then remember to give you licks, aren't you?" John Alan challenged him. "Miss Cathcart does give birthday swats, but she doesn't hit very hard." He grinned at her and was glad when she smiled back.

"I'm not afraid of anything," Simon said, tracing his finger around the circle of his inkwell. He didn't look up. "I'm not afraid of anything," he repeated, "or anybody, either," he added looking up at John Alan. "It's just that ... it's just that ... I'm ... adopted. I'm adopted and nobody knows the exact date I was born."

The room got as quiet as a church when the preacher is about to baptize somebody. Miss Cathcart's mouth began to screw up, and for a moment John Alan thought she was going to burst into tears. The old Miss Cathcart would have, but this new one turned around to her desk and sat down.

"God knows when your birthday is," Shirley Jean whispered loud enough for everybody in the room to hear. "God knows everything," she murmured. "That's what my mama says. He even knows what you're thinking before you think it."

"Well, yes," Miss Cathcart replied, getting control of her mouth at last. "Yes, God certainly does know everything, but ... but ... he doesn't always pass information on to us." There was another pause before she said, "I know what! I'll satisfy your curiosity at last! We'll start with my birthday!"

That got everybody's mind off of Simon in a hurry. They'd been begging her all year to tell them when her birthday was and how old she was. For some reason teachers never wanted to tell stuff like that, and John Alan could never figure out why. He'd been tempted to go through her employment file in his father's office and find out for himself, but that would not be keeping his nose clean. That one rule issued by his father covered an awful lot of territory.

He was as interested as everybody else in finding out her age since he was pretty sure she was lots older than Joe Bob Snow, who had just graduated from high school. Why, she was practically an old maid!

"My birthday is on the twenty-second of May," she said, writing it on the blackboard under *Defense* and next to *tris-kai-dek-a-pho-bi-a.*

"Now, if I told you that May 22 was on a Saturday the year I was born, and that I was born in a leap year, could you look at your perpetual calendar and figure out how old I am? You will have to add just a little dash of logic to the facts I gave you. Pretend you are Sherlock Holmes. The first person to figure out my age will win a savings stamp."

After football books and *Wind in the Willows,* books about Sherlock Holmes were John Alan's favorites. That was one reason he liked Paul. Paul had read every Sherlock Holmes story ever written, and so had he. He wouldn't have any trouble thinking like Sherlock. That saving stamp would be the first one in his book. He started to run his finger down the row of calendars.

"Here's one!" Jean Margaret shouted. "A May 22 on a Saturday! On calendar number six!"

"Don't tell everything you know, Jean Margaret," Miss Cathcart smiled.

She said that a lot, but most of the class couldn't remember not to do it. John Alan could, though. He'd had a lot of practice not telling things.

"Okay, okay, I see that on calendar six, too," Jimmy growled, "but I don't know what to do now that I've found it." He slammed his almanac shut. "I never win anything!"

"You're giving up too quickly, Jimmy. Think about the facts I gave you, and add to them what you can guess to be true," Miss Cathcart said slowly.

"I know the answer," Simon Green said in a voice that was little more than a whisper. John Alan was the only one who heard him, and he was nowhere near finding out when Miss Cathcart's birthday was. He looked at Simon for a minute, and then raised his own hand.

"Yes, John Alan? Do you know the answer?"

"I don't, but Simon here does," he said, jerking his thumb at Simon.

Miss Cathcart quickly covered the look of surprise on her face, but not before John Alan saw it. He was pretty sure Rachel and Simon did, too.

"How old am I, Simon?" Miss Cathcart asked, going over and putting her hand on his shoulder so she could read what he had scribbled in his Big Chief tablet.

"Well, there's just one May 22 on a Saturday that's in a leap year, and it's on calendar number twelve," he said in a very matter-of-fact tone. Every kid in the class scrambled their fingers over to calendar twelve. Sure enough, there was May 22 on a Saturday, and the February above it had twenty-nine days.

"Now, that calendar," Simon went on, sounding a lot like Mr. North, the ace detective on the radio, "like the other eleven in that section, applies to a great number of different years. But you said we needed to use Sherlock Holmes-like deductive reasoning. Since it is common knowledge that you are a first-year teacher who graduated from college last year, I deduced that you must be in your early twenties."

Miss Cathcart was smiling very broadly now, and John Alan was trying to decide whether he liked Simon or wished he'd stayed wherever it was he had come from. He'd have to think about that for a while.

"So I subtracted 21, 22, 23, and 24 from this year, 1942, and came up with 1920, 1921, 1922, and 1923 as possible years of your birth."

By this time, the rest of the class was completely lost, but John Alan saw how Simon had done it.

"I checked out those four years," Simon lectured on, "and the only one with May 22 on a Saturday that is also a leap year was 1920. So that makes 1920 the year you were born. That makes you twenty-one years, eight months, and somewhere between fifteen and twenty-nine days old." He paused to take a breath. "It will take me a little longer to get the exact number of days because of the leap years involved, but I can do it."

"I'm sure you can, Simon, I'm sure you can," Miss Cathcart told him as she walked to the front of the room and turned to look back at the class. She flashed the V for victory sign, and then began to clap her hands, and before long, all the kids had joined her, even John Alan Feester.

After the applause had stopped, Simon raised his hand again. Miss Cathcart nodded for him to go on.

"May I add one more bit of information?"

"Certainly, Simon. You have our undivided attention."

"Well, you mentioned the world's most famous private detective, Sherlock Holmes. I just wondered if you knew that you and Sir Arthur Conan Doyle, the writer who created the fictional Holmes, share the same birthday?"

Miss Cathcart did not try to hide her surprise this time. "No, Simon, I did not know that. Sir Arthur Conan Doyle was born on my birthday?"

"Not in the same year you were born, of course,"
Simon Green said with a slight smile. "Doyle was born
in 1859 and died in 1930. He didn't become 'Sir' until
1902." Simon didn't really rattle this information off
like a smarty-pants showoff. He simply stated the facts
because he thought everybody should know them.

Paul had done that a lot, too, and John Alan
looked over to see how Rachel was reacting to
Simon's Paul-like lecture. She was busy folding up a
note she had written to somebody, so he watched to
see where it got passed. When he realized it was
headed for Simon's desk, John Alan managed to grab
it away from Jean Margaret before she could pass it
on. He watched Rachel's face turn beet red as he
opened it, but she couldn't do anything about it without Miss Cathcart seeing her. The note read:

SIMON, WHAT ARE YOU DOING ON MARCH 13?
MAYBE YOU'D LIKE TO COME TO MY BIRTHDAY PARTY.
I'LL LOOK FOR YOU AT RECESS THIS AFTERNOON SO I
CAN TELL YOU ALL ABOUT IT.

It was signed "Rachel the Resister."
John Alan folded the note back up exactly the
way it had been folded in the first place, and when
Miss Cathcart wasn't looking, flipped it over on

Simon's desk. He looked over at Rachel and smirked so she wouldn't know how badly he wished that invitation had been for him. "Aid and comfort!" he mouthed at her. And just in case she couldn't read his lips, he wrote those three fatal words on a piece of paper, folded it into a nice, neat square, and dropped it on her desk on his way to the pencil sharpener.

"One more bit of trivia," Simon was rattling on. Miss Cathcart was seated on the corner of her desk, and she began to jiggle her foot like she'd had about as much of Simon Green as she wanted to hear today. John Alan saw that right away, but Simon didn't seem to notice that foot at all. He kept right on talking. He reminded John Alan of a stopped-up faucet that got unplugged and then couldn't be shut off.

"While I was skimming the calendars, I noticed Shirley Jean will be thirteen on Friday the thirteenth in 1944. That should make for an interesting birthday." He turned to see Shirley Jean's reaction to his news. "I hope you don't suffer from triskaidekophobia. That's nothing but a silly superstition with no truth in it," he added. Shirley Jean blushed and ducked her head.

"I knew about my thirteenth birthday already, Simon," she said, looking down at her desk instead of at him. "My mother figured it out when I was eight.

My birthday was on Friday the thirteenth that year, too. But I'm glad you noticed. I sure hope you'll be able to come to my party. This year, I mean." Her face was as red as the sweater she had on as she added, "You're invited in 1943 and '44, too, of course."

John Alan couldn't believe it. Simon Green, who had not said a voluntary word since the morning he walked into this class until today, who had only lived in this town a month, had already been invited to more birthday parties than he had, and he'd lived here almost half a year! Not that he'd go, of course. But he did wish he got invited sometimes.

He needed to have a talk with Simon Green, and the sooner the better!

CHAPTER 10
Encyclopedia Green

When John Alan saw Rachel walking home for lunch, he decided to have his talk with Simon Green while she wasn't around to butt in. Simon needed to be told that Rachel went around accusing perfectly normal people of being spies and traitors before he decided whether or not he wanted to go to her birthday party! He thought Simon would think her suspicions were pretty funny, and he wanted to make Simon laugh.

All those things Simon had told them in class made John Alan want him for a friend. Not the kind of friend he could ask to come to his house or anything like that, but a friend who could talk to him at

77

recess. He could remember not to let any secrets slip out. He knew he could do that.

John Alan didn't have to look for Simon because he was in the same spot he went to every recess, the base of the flagpole. He always sat on the little round patch of cement that surrounded the bottom and used the pole for a backrest while he read. When he first started doing that, some of the boys—John Alan included—teased him and tried to grab his book and hat, but the teachers on duty ran them off. It wasn't long before they left him alone.

Still, when John Alan walked up, Simon clutched his book to his chest and put his hand on his hat protectively. "Go, away, John Alan. I'm busy!" he said, looking over the tops of the thickest glasses John Alan had ever seen. He'd seen the glasses, but he hadn't realized they were so thick. The kid was as blind as Rachel, who couldn't even read the blackboard without hers!

"What you reading?" John Alan asked in what he hoped was a give-me-another-chance tone of voice. Since he wasn't pretending to be bad for the first time in a long time, he wasn't sure exactly how to act.

"Volume S of the *Encyclopedia Britannica*," Simon replied, looking off into space instead of at him. He could tell Simon was still wary of him, but it was very important to him that Simon knew there was some good in him. Paul knew that, but Paul was gone now, and John Alan needed at least one person around who knew the truth: he was not really a bad person. He would never be able to convince the other kids in the class, but Simon was new to town. He was John Alan's only chance.

"Volume S? Have you read all the rest of them up to that? Are you going to read the whole set?" John Alan ran the questions together before Simon had a chance to answer.

"I already have," Simon replied, not changing his expression or the tone of his voice. "Read the whole set, I mean. Four times." He loosened his grip on the book, and Rachel's note, which he had been using to mark his place, slipped out. John Alan recognized it immediately, but didn't say anything. "You've been here a while," Simon went on. "Tell me something. Who is it Rachel's resisting? She signed that note to me 'Rachel the Resister.' What's she mean by that?"

"You've read the whole encyclopedia four times?" John Alan asked, hoping to stay away from the subject of Rachel. "That's amazing! Really amazing! Why'd you do that?"

"My parents bought them for me so I'd stop

reading cereal boxes," Simon Green said, patting the book just like it was his favorite dog.

John Alan needed to keep him talking. "You got a dog?" he asked.

"I had one. Her fur was the same color as Rachel's hair." Rachel, again! He had to keep Simon away from the subject of Rachel.

"Must have been an Irish setter then, right? I really like Irish setters! They're my favorite kind of dog!" For once, John Alan was telling the truth.

"Yep, that's what she was, all right," Simon said wistfully. "Or is. Her name's Zinziberi. That's Latin for the roots of the ginger plant. Red hair, ginger, get it? I was reading the Z's when I got her!" he said with a big smile. The smile faded quickly and in a very flat tone he added, "I had to give Zinziberi away when we moved."

"Gee, that's awful. My father won't let me have a dog, but if I ever did get one, I know I couldn't stand to give it away. Why wouldn't they let you bring Zinziberi with you?" he asked, but what he really wanted to know was why any kid would read the backs of cereal boxes.

"Mother said she'd be too much trouble on that long a trip because she's so big and our car's so small, but I would have managed. We could have let her have the whole back seat." He looked like he was going to cry.

"When'd you learn how to read?" John Alan said, fishing for a happier subject. "I mean, it'd take about a hundred years to read the encyclopedia four times! You musta learned pretty young."

"Yep, I learned when I was three, but I didn't leave the cereal boxes till I was four. My mother says I taught myself. One morning I just picked up a cereal box and started reading the information on the back. I did that every day at breakfast. That's all I wanted to read, the backs of cereal boxes. They tried to give me books, but I wasn't interested."

"I think that's very funny," John Alan said, grinning and shaking his head. "You were probably the only kid in the world who wanted to go to the grocery store instead of the library!"

Simon smiled back at him. "As a matter of fact, that was my favorite place to read ... the cereal section of the grocery store! That was because the other shoppers would hear me ... I only read aloud in those days ... and they'd call total strangers over and get me to read for them. I was a big show-off back then. For a three-year-old kid, I could draw quite a crowd." He stopped talking, put his lips together, and stared at John Alan a minute. "I'm not boring you, am I?"

"Nope," John Alan answered with a laugh. "It takes a lot to bore me!"

"My mother says that's why I don't make friends easily ... I lecture instead of talk, she says. I ... I don't mean to do that, but I just have so much information rolling around in my head I have to get rid of some of it from time to time."

Simon Green was the weirdest kid John Alan had ever met, but he liked him. Liked him a lot. Besides, Simon hadn't been here long enough to hear all the bad rumors about him. How he bullied Miss Cathcart into making him class president, how he might have been the one who set off firecrackers in the bathroom, how he could have pushed over the outhouse with Mr. Johnson inside, how he tormented Rachel all the time.

Rachel! He needed to keep Simon away from Rachel, or she'd rat on him for sure. If he had a little more time, maybe he and Simon could become friends, but not if Rachel got to him first. He'd have to keep a close eye on Simon next recess.

The bell rang to signal the end of lunchtime, and John grabbed Simon's free hand and jerked him to his feet. Rachel's note fell to the ground, but Simon was busy tying the strings on his cap and didn't notice. John Alan picked it up and started to stuff it in his jacket pocket, but he changed his mind and handed it back to Simon. Simon smiled and nodded.

"Race you to the line," John Alan shouted before he remembered Simon was the last person to go in the room every day. "I mean ... I mean ... guess it's time to go back in now." He slowed his pace to match Simon's shuffle, but it sure was hard to move like a turtle when everybody else was running like that track star Glenn Cunningham, trying to be first in line.

They got there in time to be next-to-last and last. John Alan grinned when Simon shoved him in front of him and took last place.

Rachel, as usual, was first, but this time, John Alan was glad. The way he saw it, the further away from Simon she was, the better.

CHAPTER 11
Jeep, the Dog

When the afternoon recess bell rang, John Alan almost knocked Jean Margaret flat on her bottom trying to be the first one out the door. He'd read Rachel's note and knew she'd be heading straight for Simon Green. Jean Margaret had her pencil box in her hand when he hit her, and the contents of the box went flying all over the floor.

"You big lummox!" she squealed. "If you don't pick it up, I'll tell! I'll tell!"

He looked around frantically and saw Miss Cathcart whispering to Miss Oxley, the other fifth-grade teacher (sixth grade only had one class; fifth grade had two), and he knew for sure she would make him stay in for recess if Jean Margaret told. Miss Oxley would force her to do it. Everybody said Miss Oxley was the meanest teacher in Theodore Roosevelt Elementary School, maybe the meanest one who ever lived. But his father thought she was the best teacher in Oklahoma. He'd said so lots of times.

The last thing in the world John Alan needed was to have to stay in this recess. That would give Rachel fifteen whole minutes alone with Simon!

He grabbed up Jean Margaret's scissors, erasers, and pencils as fast as he could grab and shoved them back in her splintery wooden pencil box. By the looks of it, that box had belonged to her sixth-grade brother and maybe her seventh-grade sister, too, before it got handed down to her. It had some kind of picture on the top that had faded so much you couldn't even tell what it was.

As he handed it back to her, he remembered that fancy pencil box of Rachel's. The one Paul had stolen. The ruler on top of it was the exact blue of the sapphire ring his father had bought his mother ... no ... that his father had bought Toad ... for their tenth wedding anniversary. He tried to picture a frog with a sapphire ring on, but his mother's slender white hand popped up in his mind instead. He blinked his eyes to erase the memory of that hand and rushed out the door.

"No girls allowed!" John Alan barked as he ran up to the flagpole where Rachel was crouched down next to Simon. John Alan arrived just in time to hear her say, " ... nothing but a belligerent enigma, that's all he is!"

"Welcome to the club," Simon said with a big grin. "I just found out that *you* are the one Rachel is resisting! Wouldn't you know it? The only two people in the class I want for friends, and you hate each other! Have a seat at the bargaining table. I, a personal envoy from the president of the United States, have been sent to negotiate a truce in the Rachel Resistance!" He looked back and forth between them and continued to smile broadly.

John Alan had no choice. He wanted Simon for a friend, so he sat down. He had no idea what all Rachel had blabbed. He knew one thing for sure: he was the "belligerent enigma" she was carrying on about when he came up. She had called him that several times lately. "You belligerent enigma!" she'd yelled as she zoomed past him on her bike the other day. He'd hollered "aid and comfort" back at her before he jumped on his own bike and rode off.

Just as Simon started to speak again, Jeep,

Rachel's dog, trotted down the sidewalk that surrounded the school. Jeep was very careful not to let a paw touch the school ground itself. He had been run off so many times by the teachers on duty, he knew better than to cross that invisible barrier between the real world and the world of school. Rachel froze and pretended not to see him because she knew if she made eye contact, he'd forget the rules and get in trouble. Again. One time Miss Oxley even called the dogcatcher!

"That's my dog," she whispered to Simon. "But don't look at him! He gets in bad trouble if he comes on the playground." She began to draw a horse in the dust just like Paul used to do, except hers was flat and boring. Paul's horses always looked like they were moving.

A squirrel scampered down a tree on the other side of the street, and Jeep took off after it.

"What's his name?" Simon asked. "Your dog, I mean. I assume you are not acquainted with the squirrel." He smiled at his own joke.

"Jeep!" John Alan blurted out before Rachel could open her mouth. "His name's Jeep! And he can do great tricks. If Rachel's father asks him if he'd rather be a dead dog or a Democrat, Jeep falls on his back, sticks all four feet up in the air, and lets his tongue loll out."

"How'd you know that?" Rachel asked, erasing the dust horse with one sweep of her hand. "How'd you know about Jeep's trick? You've never even met my dog!"

"I know about everybody's dogs," John Alan said with a shrug. "I learn their names right off . . . their tricks, too. . . . In case . . . in case my father ever lets me get one. Don't want to name my dog the same as anybody else's."

"Well, in addition to his many tricks, Jeep is a great judge of character," Rachel bragged. "He can tell good people from bad people with just one sniff. My father says Jeep is never wrong, so you better hope he never smells you, John Alan Feester, because . . ."

"I had a dog," Simon interrupted her. "Told John Alan all about her at lunch today. Her name's Zinziberi and her fur is exactly the color of your hair." He gave a sigh and looked at his watch. "It's almost time for her to eat. I keep my watch set on Eastern Standard Time so I'll know when it's time to feed her."

"But since you're not the one who feeds her anymore, why do you do that, Simon?" Rachel asked.

"I don't know," he replied as he looked at her hair and sighed again. "I just do." For a minute John Alan thought Simon was going to pat Rachel on the head and scratch her behind her ears. Evidently Rachel thought so too, because she quickly scooted away from Simon, and in the process almost ended up in John Alan's lap. It almost looked like she wanted him to protect her. He laughed when she scooted back away again.

"Now about your dog, Rachel," Simon said, launching into his lecture tone again. "Was your Jeep named for Eugene the Jeep?"

"Eugene the Jeep? I . . . I don't think so. Who's Eugene the Jeep?"

"A cartoon character . . . in Thimble Theater. That particular strip appears in newspapers rather than comic books. Thimble Theater was the first comic strip I ever read," he rambled on, looking off into space and chewing on the strings of his green cap as if remembering that really made him happy. "If he were a pup instead of a full grown dog, I would have assumed your family named him for the army vehicle that is becoming more and more popular these days, the one made by Willys-Overland Motors. Jeep is its nickname. From GP for General Purpose vehicle."

Rachel and John Alan looked at each other again. Was there anything this walking encyclopedia didn't know?

"Oh ... oh ... I get it," John Alan stammered. "GP sounds like Jeep when you say it out loud."

"That's very interesting," Rachel added. "I guess. I mean, if a person is interested in army vehicles."

"Well, I'm interested in army vehicles!" John Alan assured Simon, punching him on the arm. "Been reading a lot about them lately! I started reading the war news in the paper every day when I found out the Rose Bowl was being moved." He saw Rachel's eyebrows go up when he said that, so he added, "Rachel was the first one to tell me about the Rose Bowl. She always knows war news before anybody else because her father has a Teletype." It was coming back to him—how to be good was coming back.

"Which brings us back to war again," Simon said in a very official tone. "I thought the two of you were mortal enemies," Simon said, looking back and forth between them, "yet here we are having a peaceful but lively discussion about dogs and military vehicles. May we assume that you are willing to at least try a truce in the Rachel Resistance? We only ask that you cease hostilities until the real war ... World War II ... is over. Surely that will be in the near future. What do you think?"

John Alan and Rachel stared at each other for a whole minute without saying a word. Simon Green was right. The two of them had been having a normal conversation, an ordinary discussion without either one of them attacking the other. It was possible. A truce was possible.

"If he'll stop saying 'aid and comfort, aid and comfort' every time he seems me," Rachel said looking at the ground instead of either of them. John Alan could tell by the blank look on Simon's face she hadn't told him about the eavesdropping, and he was glad about that. But maybe she was so busy telling Simon all about her stupid old birthday party she hadn't mentioned it. She sure hadn't mentioned any birthday party to him yet.

"Will she stop calling me names like 'belligerent'?" John Alan challenged, trying not to sound like a person who was eager to fight. "Or enigma, either," he added, remembering he needed to look that one up in the dictionary when he got home. He couldn't very well be an enigma if he didn't even know what it meant.

"I'm sure you both can abide by a few rules, sort of like the Geneva Convention," Simon told them.

"What's the Geneva Convention?" Rachel wanted to know.

"Check your *Weekly Reader,* Rachel," John Alan said, disgusted with her ignorance. "You must be really stupid not to remember about the Geneva Convention!" Then he remembered the truce. "I mean ... I mean ..." He looked to Simon for help and received an encouraging nod. "What I meant to say was that in December one whole edition of *Weekly Reader* was devoted to Switzerland. They talked a bunch about the Geneva Convention. It has to do with red crosses on ambulances and things like that."

"I throw those dumb *Weekly Readers* away the day we get them," Rachel snipped. "I hate *Weekly Readers* almost as much as I hate ..." She saw Simon watching her, so she clamped her mouth shut. "Paul liked them though, so there must be something good about them. He saved every single issue. He even talked his father into letting him take them with him to California."

"I save them, too," John Alan told her. He hesitated a minute before he added, "I'll ... I'll loan you mine ... if you don't mind touching something that belongs to me. I don't have cooties, you know."

"Okay, I'll drop by your house after school today and pick it up!"

"No!" John Alan hollered. "I mean ... No need to go to all that trouble. I'll bring it to school tomorrow." This truce business was going to be tricky since he wasn't allowed to invite anybody to his house. His father had instructed him to tell people they couldn't come in because there was no adult there. Lots of kids had that rule, so they would accept that, he thought.

"See," Simon beamed, "that wasn't hard, was it? You're both just going to have to break a few old habits."

The bell rang, and John Alan and Rachel bumped heads trying to be the first one standing up. They glared at each other, then raced for the line like their coattails were on fire. They pushed and shoved all the way to the sidewalk finish line. John Alan won, but when he saw Simon frowning at him from the back of the line, he stepped back and let Rachel take first place. Simon smiled again and flashed them the V for victory sign.

CHAPTER 12
Daddy Warbucks' Mansion

When John Alan Feester, Jr., traded Rachel Elizabeth Dalton a fried chicken drumstick for half a peanut butter sandwich the next day *and* gave her his only napkin, the other kids in 5B knew something was up. The entire morning had passed without a single rude exchange between the two of them. Even Miss Cathcart, who seemed quite distracted these days, noticed the absence of hostilities. But she was so busy running to the door to whisper to Miss Oxley that she didn't take the time to comment.

Since their school did not have a lunchroom, everybody, including the teachers, ate their sack lunches at their desks, but this day Miss Cathcart was eating standing up in the doorway. So was Miss Oxley, who could keep an eagle eye on her classroom from any spot on the planet.

"Go right on out to the playground the minute you finish your lunch," Miss Cathcart commanded as she pointed to the door with half a bologna sandwich. "The sooner the better!" Since she usually tried to make everybody chew ten times before they swallowed, and she always made the whole class wait until everybody finished to go outside, this was a change—a big change. But they weren't sure what it meant.

John Alan, Simon, and Rachel were the first three to finish, and they dashed for the flagpole the minute they got their desktops cleaned.

"We could go someplace else if you want to," Simon told them after he'd caught his breath. "The only reason I came here was for the backrest, but since I don't have to read anymore ..."

"Let's go to Daddy Warbucks' then!" Rachel shouted as she took off for the four very old horse apple trees that huddled on the far corner of the lot.

"What'd you call this place?" Simon asked as he

plopped down on the ground between two giant roots that stuck half in, half out of the dry, dusty ground. The four trees had been planted in the shape of a baseball diamond except they were only about three feet apart. The tree that could have been home plate was the largest and had the most tree-root divisions.

"Daddy Warbucks'," Rachel explained kneeling between two fat roots on the tree next to his. "Paul named it when we were in first grade. Paul names everything, even wars." She smirked at John Alan. "With all these roots dividing the ground up into rooms, we pretended it was the mansion Little Orphan Annie got to live in after Daddy Warbucks adopted her!" John Alan frowned at her when she said "adopted." Didn't she remember what Simon said about being adopted and not even knowing when his birthday was? He sure remembered the things people said about their fathers and mothers.

"Bet you never listened to that stupid program, did ya, Simon?" John Alan jumped in, trying to steer the subject away from orphans. "That was a dumb girl program!"

"Bet you listen to Captain Midnight though," Rachel countered. "He took Annie's place on the radio. Every kid in Oklahoma listens to Captain Midnight," she sneered, knowing full well John Alan didn't.

"We don't own a radio," Simon admitted with a shrug. "So I've never listened to any of those programs."

"You don't own a radio?" Rachel and John Alan said at the same time. Then they both looked around to see if anybody else had heard them. They were sure this was not the kind of information Simon would want spread around. His family must be as poor as church mice if they couldn't even afford a radio.

"My father thinks listening to a radio corrupts the intellectual process. He says reading is the only real way to learn. School is necessary for the development of social skills, he says, and to expose oneself to the opinion of others. But he doesn't believe in radio listening."

"You don't own a radio," John Alan repeated as if Simon had just told them he had moved to Oklahoma from Mars. "I didn't know there was anybody who didn't have a radio."

"Well, we don't," Simon sighed, "but sometimes I wish we did. Tell me about this Captain Midnight, Rachel. What's he the captain of? Is he smart?"

"Only about the smartest person who ever lived. He even knew Pearl Harbor was gonna get bombed before it happened."

"How could he know that? He's a fictional character, isn't he? Nobody knew Pearl Harbor was going to be bombed," Simon replied just as the bell rang, ending noon recess.

"Remember you're talking to a girl who thought *I* had something to do with Pearl Harbor," John Alan reminded him as they all sprang to their feet. "Aid and comfort!" he shouted, throwing three little words at her and instantly breaking their truce.

***

When Rachel finally made her way to Daddy Warbucks' mansion during afternoon recess, Simon began to press for a new truce. He and John Alan had headed straight for the trees when they left the building, but it had taken Rachel quite a while to decide she was going to join them.

"John Alan wants to say he's sorry," Simon said as he punched him in the ribs with his elbow. "Don't you want to say you're sorry, John Alan?"

"I am not ... well ... I guess ... yeah, I guess. I'm sorry I said 'aid and comfort' Rachel," he grinned as he kicked a rock into one of her root-marked rooms.

"He did it again, Simon! He said that on purpose!"

"But you are willing to give him another chance

not to say it, aren't you, Rachel?" he asked, pointing his finger at her and elbowing John Alan again at the same time. "Sure you are! The world's got all the wars it can handle right now. Take your seats, please," he directed, and they all sat down. "When the bell rang, you, Rachel, were about to tell me about Captain Midnight. John Alan wants to know, too, since he's never listened to him either. Right, John Alan? You want Rachel to tell us all about Captain Midnight, don't you?" He reached over and punched him in the arm, and John Alan shrugged his shoulders.

"Well, Captain Midnight's an airplane pilot, and he's head of this really neat Secret Squadron. If you send off coupons from boxes of Ovaltine, you get a membership certificate and an official Captain Midnight Code-O-Graph badge so you can decode the secret messages. Everybody in our class belongs to the Secret Squadron ... everybody except John Alan, that is." She scooped up a handful of leaves and dirt and dropped it all on John Alan's newly polished shoes.

"Why would I— " John Alan began, clenching both fists.

"I know what!" Rachel interrupted. "I'm sure listening to Captain Midnight just once would not damage your brain very much, Simon. How about you coming over to my house after school today? The program's on from four-thirty until four-forty-five. I can explain things better while we're listening." She turned to John Alan, who was dusting off his shoes with a handkerchief. "I'd invite you, too, John Alan," she said sweetly, "but I know you wouldn't come since you think Captain Midnight's dumb."

"Well, I used to say that, but ... but ... I changed my mind!" He was picturing all the alone time Rachel would have with Simon if he didn't go with them, time when she could blurt out all sorts of bad information about him. "I'll come, too, and you can explain the program to both of us at the same time. Thanks for the invite!" He grinned as she pinched her lips together and pulled the corners of her mouth way down, but didn't reply.

"That's a great idea!" Simon interjected. "This'll be a great way to work on your truce. Both of you right there in the same room listening to the same program." He stood up and solemnly shook hands with both of them. "Miss Cathcart asked me to stay after school and help bundle the newspapers, but that won't take long. If you'll tell me how to get to your house, I'll come over as soon as I'm finished."

"I'll stay and help you! That way we can walk to my house together!"

"Me, too," John Alan chimed in. "It'll go lots quicker with all three of us helping!"

Rachel put her hands on her hips and glared at him again, but she didn't say another word. She was trapped, and she knew it. John Alan had won again! He flashed her the V for victory sign.

CHAPTER 13
Serving Uncle Sam

"This won't take long, especially with three of you to help," Miss Cathcart said, looking back and forth between Rachel and John Alan with a question mark on her face. She was certain the two of them had never voluntarily worked together on any project, but by the way he was smiling at them, it looked like Simon had something to do with them being here now.

"Take the bundles of newspapers out of that box, and be really careful not to break the strings they're tied with. Stack them on the shelves over the radiators. I'll measure the height of each person's stack, then we'll put them in Joseph O'Connor's wagon over there. He's outside dusting erasers for me, but he volunteered to roll the wagon down to the Legion Hall when he finished. That's the collection center, and his father has a key since he's the post commander. Must be where Joseph gets his desire to serve."

"Joe's daddy was the youngest World War I veteran in Caddo County to register for the draft!" Rachel informed them in her late-breaking news bulletin voice. John Alan rolled his eyes at Simon, but Simon just grinned. "Mr. O'Connor won't be forty till this summer! My daddy wrote about it in the paper last week," she prattled on. "My daddy's going to be forty-five pretty soon, so I think he's way too old to go to war, but he still had to register for the draft."

"Almost everybody has to register now," Miss Cathcart told them as she straightened the bundles in neat, even rows. "Even the president himself. Nobody knows how old is 'too old.' Not yet, anyway. It ... it depends on how many we lose...." She stared down at a January 2 headline. " 'Manila Falls: Death Toll High,' " she read out loud, but her voice trailed off to a whisper at the end. "That's where Dave Obert is, remember?" She shook her head as if the motion would make the sad thoughts fall out her ears.

"Get my ruler from my desk, would you, Simon? And the yellow record sheet. I'll measure, you and

John Alan can move the bundles to the wagon, and Rachel can write down the number of inches collected next to each person's name. Remember, the one with the most inches wins a savings stamp, so be sure you get them down right."

"It's really strange to think about these newspapers being turned into lunchboxes or wastebaskets," Simon said, running his fingers over the page and getting newsprint all over them. "That's what they do with some of them, you know. Make things they used to make out of metal so they can use the metal to make airplanes and boats for the navy." He chewed his lip as he added, "Hard to imagine . . . cardboard lunchboxes and wastepaper baskets make out of waste paper. Like you said, war changes everything, doesn't it?"

"It does, indeed, Simon. War makes people turn 'plowshares into swords.' That's from the Bible. Blades of steel that plowed up pretty flower gardens get turned into bayonets to kill people." She blinked back tears and swallowed hard. Simon and Rachel exchanged a puzzled looked, but John Alan stared down at another headline: "Pearl Harbor Death Toll Grows." He knew why Miss Cathcart was talking about gardens and plows. She was remembering Joe Bob Snow and that can of dirt from his grandmother's garden. So was he.

"I'm sorry kids," she said shaking her head again. "I get carried away sometimes. It's just that I feel so . . . so . . . useless these days. Like I ought to be doing something else . . . something bigger."

John Alan started to say something—something about the men who were serving our country—but he changed his mind. Simon hadn't talked much about his father, so he didn't know if he was in the military or not. But then, John Alan hadn't said a word about his mother, so he wasn't about to ask. Rachel never stopped rattling on about her parents, both of them, but she was a girl and girls told everything they knew. For once he was glad his father made him keep his mouth shut about family matters.

"We're going to have to work a lot harder on our newspaper drive from now on," Miss Cathcart told them when they were finished measuring and loading. "Miss Oxley's room had four wagonloads, and we barely have one! I know it may not seem very important . . . collecting newspapers . . . but it is. Everything we can do . . . every single thing will shorten the time our boys have to fight!" She started to tear up again. "Thanks for your help! See you tomorrow!" She turned her back to them and snuffled into her handkerchief. She always carried a handkerchief these days.

None of them could think of anything to say to her, so they pulled on their coats, gloves, and caps and left without telling her good-bye.

They tiptoed past 5A, Miss Oxley's room, to keep her from looking up and shouting, "Stop the noise, all girls and boys!" She yelled that at anybody she saw, even if they weren't making any noise at all.

"Well, I guess we gave old Odious Oxley the slip that time," John Alan said after the big wooden door snapped shut behind them. He started calling her Odious when that word was on their vocabulary list. Now every kid in the fifth grade called her that. It was fun to say, and since it meant "deserving of hatred; hated or abhorred" they were sure the word was created to describe Miss Oxley. "They should put her in charge of the war," he added as he picked up an old ice cream bar stick and began to rake it down Johnson's picket fence. "Bet she could make old Hitler holler uncle."

Simon and Rachel nodded their agreement as Rachel started jumping the cracks in the sidewalk.

"Step on a crack, break your mother's back!" she began to chant. Simon began to hop and chant along behind her. "Come on, John Alan ... do it with us! Don't want to break your mother's ..." She stopped so suddenly that Simon almost ran her down. John

Alan knew why she'd stopped. She'd stopped because she remembered his mother's back could no longer be broken since she was dead.

"Last one to the Flying Red Horse is a rotten egg," John Alan yelled as he threw the ice cream stick at her and took off running. Simon caught the stick in the air and broke it in two before he handed it to Rachel.

CHAPTER 14
Simon, the Sailor, and Jay

Until they were catching their breath in front of the Flying Red Horse, John Alan had forgotten what Rachel had hollered that day in her father's office, the thing about Mr. Johnson being a spy, too. What was it she said? Something about Benedict Arnold, he thought, but he wasn't sure. Then he spotted the little sign that hung down on two chains, the sign which read "B. Arnold Johnson, Proprietor."

"Hey, Rachel, you know everything," he taunted.

"What's the B stand for in Mr. B. Arnold Johnson's name?"

"Beauregard," she replied, without looking at either him or the sign. "And don't tell me that was the name of a general in the Civil War, because Paul already told me that. Paul knows everything there is to know about the Civil War!"

"Yeah, but I remember you saying ..."

"Simon, bet you know a lot about the Civil War, don't you?" she interrupted before John Alan could get his question out. Simon, of course, launched into a Civil War lecture that lasted all the way to Rachel's house.

John Alan decided to save his question for another day, but he was determined to find out the answer.

***

"Well, loopin' loops!" Rachel's mother said in imitation of Captain Midnight. "Who have we here?" She had just rounded the corner from the kitchen and spotted three kids in her living room, two of whom had never been there before. She had a glass of Ovaltine in one hand and a jelly sandwich on a plate in the other. "Has the Secret Squadron been advised of this surprising development?" she prattled on. She sounded just like Rachel. John Alan watched a smile as big as Texas spread over her face when she recognized him. It made him feel warm all over. "Why, how in the world are you, John Alan Feester, Jr.?" she asked. "I'm delighted to see you!" She transferred the smile to Rachel as she added, "You boys just throw your jackets on that chair. We gave all our extra hangers to the scrap metal drive last week. The war's even changed our good manners, hasn't it? Speaking of which, I don't believe I've met this young man, Rachel."

"Simon Green, that's my mother," Rachel muttered as she headed for the radio and flipped on the dial. John Alan could tell she was still peeved at him for butting his way in. He looked at his watch. It was 4:23.

"Green ... Green? You must be Sylvie Green's son," Mrs. Dalton said, putting her hand out in response to the one Simon stuck forward. "I met Sylvie at the Civil Defense League. She's a lovely woman!"

"Yes, Sylvie's my mother," Simon replied, shaking her hand solemnly. John Alan thought he looked like a preacher at the door of the church.

"And what a nice gentlemen she's raised," Mrs. Dalton said. That was the kind of silly thing John Alan's mother used to say. She was big on his being a gentleman at all times, for all the good it did him.

She still left, didn't she? Even though he had tried, really tried to do everything she wanted him to do.

"Well, I guess I'd better triple my jelly sandwich recipe," Mrs. Dalton said with a happy smile. His mother had always had a snack waiting for him when he got home from school, too. It was the time of day he missed her most. He nodded at Rachel's pretty mother, but he didn't say anything.

Then he watched as Mrs. Dalton's smile was replaced by that same look all the mothers had given him since he'd moved to this crummy town. She didn't ask *him* whose son *he* was, did she? You didn't ask somebody whose son he was when his mother was dead. He was about to decide coming to Rachel's house was a big mistake. That he ought to leave before he did something stupid. Like cry, maybe. Then Jeep charged into the room and jumped straight into John Alan's arms.

"Hey, there, Jeep! Good dog! Good dog! Good grief!" he laughed as he tried to pat Jeep's head. The wildly excited dog was wiggling so much that John Alan had to drop to his knees to keep his balance. He grabbed Jeep's ears and gave them a good scratching while Jeep licked his face from ear to ear and then barked several happy yelps.

"Will you look at that?" Mrs. Dalton cried. "I

haven't seen Jeep that happy since the last time he saw Paul. Paul was Jeep's favorite human in the world. That poor dog's really been moping since he moved. I'm so glad to see him happy again."

"Rachel told us her father thinks Jeep's a great judge of character," Simon said, flashing a V for victory sign at John Alan, who was giving Jeep's belly a good rubdown.

"That's true," Mrs. Dalton smiled with a nod to Rachel. "Mr. Dalton says that dog's got the best nose in the county, even keener than Rachel's, and she can identify peanut butter cookies from half a mile away."

"Maybe Jeep's got a cold and his sniffer's stopped up," Rachel snipped as she observed Jeep's instant friendship with John Alan through narrowed eyes.

Rachel was going to be harder to convince he was good than Jeep had been, he knew that for a fact. "Come on down here with us," John Alan told them. "There's room for everybody. What a dog! What a great dog!"

Mrs. Dalton was beaming at him again. "Rachel, come in the kitchen and help me with the snacks. Won't take long. There's always commercials at the first of the program anyway." Rachel followed her mother, but she walked backwards all the way so she could watch Jeep and John Alan as long as possible. Just before the swinging door snapped together, he saw her shrug her shoulders and throw her hands in the air.

"We're ready to learn about Captain Midnight," Simon announced between bites from his sandwich a few minutes later. "Aren't we, J.A.? Hey, J.A. sounds like Jay . . . just like G.P. sounds like Jeep. Think I'll start calling you J.A.!"

John Alan, whose only nickname had been "Toad," bit into his sandwich, sipped his Ovaltine, and smiled. "Sure, Simon. I'd like that."

"Well, Simon . . . and you, too, *J.A.* . . ." Rachel said with a bit of a smirk, "you can mostly tell who's the good guys and who's the bad from their voices." She seemed happy, as usual, to know things other people did not. "You can ask me questions, but only during the commercials!"

The day's exciting adventure flew by, and when the program was over, even John Alan had to agree "Captain Midnight" was great fun to listen to.

"Too bad you can't hear him every day, Simon," Rachel told him as she stroked Sally Cat. Sally had joined them during a commercial. "Bet if you begged real hard, your folks would change their minds."

"Actually, it's just my mom who decides things now," Simon said, picking up a pillow on the couch and punching his fist into it over and over again. It was a pillow Rachel's grandmother had brought them from the World's Fair in Chicago. It had "The World of Tomorrow" stitched in pink on a black background. Feathers popped out one corner, but Simon didn't seem to notice. "My dad's on the USS *Washington*," he said in a voice all pinched up at both ends. "That's a battleship, you know. He's in the navy."

John Alan didn't know how to respond to this news, and he could tell Rachel didn't either. Simon was the first friend they had whose father was actually *in* the war. Rachel's father was too old—at least for now—and John Alan's father was exempt from the draft because of his job as superintendent of schools. They looked at Simon and then at each other.

"Gee, Simon, you hadn't told us that before!" John Alan said just as he remembered he had not mentioned one of his parents, either. Boys didn't tell everything they knew like girls did. He knew that. Besides that, Simon hadn't said a word to either one of them about anything until today.

"Anybody need more to eat?" Rachel's mother broke in, getting them all off the hook. "I've got a half jar of jelly left! They haven't started rationing jelly yet, but from what your father tells me, it won't be long now."

"I've started a list of things that are rationed," Rachel informed them, running to get the list from her notebook. They looked it over and talked a while about why they thought particular things were going to be hard to get. John Alan kept looking at his watch. He needed to get home, but he didn't want to be the first to go. Rachel seemed to be taking the truce business seriously, but he still didn't want to leave her alone with Simon. Finally, Simon announced he needed to go.

"Why don't I walk you home, Simon?" John Alan suggested quickly. That way they could both leave at the same time. He wasn't sure he could trust Rachel. Not yet, anyway.

"Sure thing, J.A. I'd enjoy the company of a friend!"

For the second time that day, John Alan felt warm all over.

CHAPTER 15
Simon's Spots

John Alan got to school early the next morning so that he could capture Simon before Rachel did. He scanned the playground for him until it was time to go in the building, but Simon never came. His desk was still empty when the final bell rang. Rachel was so busy reading something written on pages from a Big Chief tablet that she didn't even seem to notice Simon's absence. John Alan tried all kinds of tricks to get her attention, but she wouldn't look up.

"Well, class," Miss Cathcart said when they had taken their seats, "I'm sorry to report that Simon Green has the red measles."

"*Owww,* I bet they're *German* measles, Miss Cathcart!" Shirley Jean squealed. "Bet a German spy gave 'em to him! I saw that in a movie once! It was all about something called 'germ warfare.' That's where they give people diseases on purpose! This German spy—"

"Now, Shirley Jean," Miss Cathcart interrupted, "I hardly think Simon's measles are the result of germ warfare. First of all, there are no German spies around here—"

"You don't know that for sure," Jean Margaret piped up. "Captain Midnight says—"

"There are spies, traitors, and saboteurs all around us!" Stanley broke in.

"And the spies they'd send to Apache would be Germans because Germans look like us! In California, all the spies are Japanese. My father told me that! I'll bet my Captain Midnight Code-O-Graph badge there's at least one German spy right here in Apache! He may be peeking in our window right now!" Every head in the room whipped toward the windows, but all they saw was poor old Mr. Snow, lugging some wastebaskets out to the trash.

"Mr. Snow's not a spy!" Kenneth Stumbling Bear informed the class. Kenneth didn't talk very often, so when he did, everybody listened. "Joe Bob's already in the United States Army, and Mr. Snow's signing for Jack so he can go, too. Jack's gonna turn seventeen next Saturday. My brother's going to his party."

John Alan looked to see how Miss Cathcart reacted when she heard Joe Bob's name, and sure enough she was pulling out her handkerchief again. He wondered if she had been invited to Jack's birthday party. He wished he had been.

"Mr. Johnson at the Flying Red Horse!" Stanley exclaimed. "He could be a spy! Everybody knows he's un-American! Throws rocks at dogs! Never flies a flag! Might have even changed his name! What if we found out his real name was Wolfgang von Hitler?"

"Now, class," Miss Cathcart commanded sternly, "you must settle down this minute, and let me get back to what Dr. Inman said about Simon's measles." She paced back and forth as she went on. "We are all sorry for Simon, but as you know, measles are very contagious." Everybody started pulling up shirtsleeves and pant legs to check for spots.

"Dr. Inman believes these are the hard measles, which are the more serious kind. The three-day measles, also known as the German measles," she paused to nod at Shirley Jean, "are usually quite mild."

She stopped pacing and sat down at her desk. "I

myself have not had the hard measles," she admitted slowly. "I discussed this with the other teachers and the principal before school. Mrs. Kardokus says your class had a heavy epidemic of hard measles when you were in the third grade, so many of you are immune. How many of you think you've had the hard measles? Raise your hands, please."

Eighteen of the twenty kids in the class, including John Alan and Rachel, raised their hands. John Alan rubbed his stomach as he remembered his mother reading him *Wind in the Willows* as he lay on his bed in his blacked-out room. Even though it was summertime, she'd made a tent out of a heavy wool blanket and sat under it so the flashlight she needed to read by would not let a single ray of light into his room.

"Well, I and the two of you who didn't raise your hands need to be on the lookout for spots and fever. Be sure to remember to tell your parents that when you get home tonight."

"I didn't know teachers ever got kid stuff," Patsy Gail giggled. "You gonna tell your mama to look for spots, too?"

"I'm afraid I'll have to since I still live at home," Miss Cathcart sighed. "Oh, yes, I forgot to mention the incubation period is seven to fourteen days, but most people come down with them in about ten. These measles can hurt your eyes if you're not careful," she cautioned. "Dark curtains on the windows and no reading at all for at least two weeks."

"We already got dark curtains," Stanley told her. "My ma stitched them up last week. For when the Germans try to bomb us after they bomb Cyril."

"Now, Stanley, I don't believe—" Miss Cathcart began, but John Alan interrupted her. It was the first time he'd done that in a long time, but he couldn't keep quiet any longer.

"Simon's hands will fall off if he has to go that long without a book in them!" he told her. "We got to think of ways to help him!"

"He can listen to the radio," Jean Margaret suggested.

John Alan whipped his head around to give Rachel the old evil eye so she wouldn't spill the beans. The way he saw it, there was no reason for the whole class to know any more of Simon's private business than they already knew. When she saw his look, Rachel put her hand down, but she gave him the evil eye back.

"I'm quite certain Simon's mother will be able to keep him occupied," Miss Cathcart said as she began to pass out their spelling papers. "Now we need to get occupied, too. Write each word you missed five times on the back of your paper. Those who had perfect papers may have free time as long as you stay in your seat."

John Alan, who hadn't missed a word, ripped a page from his tablet and, for the first time in his life, started writing a note to a girl. Rachel, who also had a perfect paper, was still reading the Big Chief tablet pages. He wondered what she found so interesting that it made her forget about Simon.

CHAPTER 16
Small-Town Truth

"Dear Rachel," John Alan began his note, but after he looked at that a minute, he tore that sheet up and got another one. "Rachel," he began again. That was better. "Meet me at Daddy Warbucks' at recess so we can discuss Simon's measles!" He studied it a while and decided to change the exclamation point into a question mark so it didn't sound so bossy, but when he did, you could tell it had been changed. He tore that sheet up, too, and started over again. This time he wrote, "Could you please meet me at Daddy Warbucks' at recess?" He thought for a moment and then he added, "Truce, remember? J.A.F."

He folded it up in a neat square and printed "R.E.D." on it. The minute he looked at his finished product, he realized he had made another mistake, but it was too late to start over again. It was time for the recess bell. He'd have to pass it on and take his chances. It wasn't his fault her dumb initials spelled out the name that made her so mad.

Oh, well. If she didn't come, he'd take care of Simon by himself.

* * *

She came, but he could see she had the "bee in her bonnet" he expected since she was fighting mad.

"You just can't stand it, can you? Just had to put R.E.D. on that note, didn't you?"

"Aw, Rachel, I didn't mean anything by it! Those are your initials, aren't they? Blame your parents! They named you, not me! It's not like I called you *Red* out loud." He made the mistake of grinning when he said that.

"I wish Simon could hear you! He'd know you're doing it on purpose! What happened to our truce, huh?"

"It's Simon we're here to talk about, and we don't have long to do it. How we goin' to help him?"

"I have a plan," Rachel told him in that same I-know-it-all tone of voice she always used with him. "First of all, I can take Jeep to visit him. Jeep loves to go to houses he's never been to before." She narrowed her eyes at John Alan, who never invited anybody to his house. "They would both enjoy that a lot!"

John Alan could just see the three of them— Simon, Rachel, and Jeep—rolling around in a blacked-out room, having a great time. Without him.

"Well," he muttered, "Jeep'd be happier if it was me you were visiting. I think I need to go along to keep Jeep company. He likes me best, you know!"

"And I can get my mother to talk Simon's mother into letting him listen to one of our radios!" she went right on as if he hadn't said a word. "My mother and Simon's mother are friends, and that's more than you can say!" she added triumphantly.

Then she remembered again.

"Oh, John Alan, I'm sorry!" She put her hand over her mouth and looked like she was about to cry. "I'm so used to jabbing back at you that I ... I ... That was mean, a really mean thing to say. I forgot! I'm always forgetting about your mother being dead!" Then she gave him the same look her mother had given him yesterday. He was sick of getting that look from people. It made him want to throw up.

In fact, he wanted to throw up all over Rachel

right now, but instead he asked her a question. A question that popped out of his mouth before he even knew he was asking it out loud instead of just thinking it.

"Have you ever heard any single living soul in this crummy town even mention my mother?" He threw his head back and looked up at the topmost leaf on the tallest tree in Daddy Warbucks' mansion so he wouldn't have to look at her when she answered. If she answered.

It took her a while.

"Sure they do, John Alan," she said slowly. "But not when you're around, of course. I think . . . I think . . . from what I heard when I was eavesdropping on my folks one night . . . all the grownups kind of agreed that when you and your father got here, nobody would talk about your mother until you or your father did. We heard about her being dead before you even moved here. You know how everybody in this town knows everybody else's business. I think . . . I think at first people did it to be nice . . . and then the war got everybody worrying more about their own problems . . . all those stars in everybody's windows. . . ." She traced her finger up and down the roots of her biggest room. Finally she said, "Do you want to talk about her now?"

"No! I don't ever want to talk about her! Not ever!" he shouted as he turned and pounded on the trunk of his tree with both fists. He hollered so loud that a bunch of fifth-grade boys, who were playing crack-the-whip nearby, stopped in the middle of the crack to come over and see what was going on.

Rachel jumped up and started beating on her tree with both fists, too. "I know I can hit it more times than you before the bell rings!" she yelled. "You may think you're faster than me, you big fat enigma, but you're not!"

"Oh, they're just at each other again," Stanley said, and the boys went back to their game.

John Alan gave her a grateful nod. "What's an enigma?" he asked softly. "You keep calling me that. Can't be one if I don't know what it is."

"A riddle. A puzzling problem."

He thought for a minute before he replied, "That's me, all right."

"You can go over to Simon's house with Jeep and me," Rachel said, wiping the tree bark off her hands. "We can take one of our radios."

"You really think your mother can talk Mrs. Green into letting Simon pollute his mind?"

"Sure," Rachel said, "my mother can do anything . . ." she started, but then she got quiet again.

He knew she was remembering what she'd said about his mother. He was glad she'd said it, though, glad she'd brought the subject up. At least he knew now why nobody ever asked about his ... Toad. He wished he'd known that a long time ago, about little towns and all. It would have saved him a lot of trouble trying to avoid their questions if he'd known they weren't going to ask any.

"Why don't you come home with me after school and we'll ask," Rachel was saying. "We could even listen to 'Captain Midnight' ... if you wanted to, that is."

"Truce?" John Alan asked, flashing her the V for victory sign.

"Truce," Rachel said, making V's with both hands. "Meet me in front of the Flying Red Horse after school, okay?"

"Okay," John Alan replied. He was glad she picked that spot. First of all, he knew that was the place she always met Paul. He'd seen them there every day as he was walking home alone. Second, that little sign under the Flying Red Horse would remind him to ask her about B. Arnold Johnson, his fellow spy!

CHAPTER 17
Bad Blood

"I know it sounds dumb now, John Alan, but at the time it made sense. At least, it did to me," Rachel said, her voice trailing off a little at the end. "Paul told me all about what a rotten spy Benedict Arnold was, how he even fooled George Washington. So when I was looking for more spies and traitors ... other than *you*, that is ..." She looked to see if he was grinning at her, but he wasn't.

"It's okay, Rachel. I know what it's like ... making things look the way you want them to look, even if you ... if you know those pictures aren't real. I do that myself. It's more fun than thinking about ... about other things."

"Well, anyway, everybody in town knows Mr. Johnson is a bad person. He never flies a flag, and he throws rocks at dogs, even little puppies. I . . . I always thought that was why his outhouse got pushed over with him in it," she said, stopping to look John Alan in the eyes. "I always thought that . . . that somebody who really liked dogs did it." He knew she thought he pushed that outhouse over, but he just shrugged his shoulders and smiled.

"Don't tell everything you know," he said in imitation of Miss Cathcart, who told that to somebody in their class every single day. "Get back to the B. Arnold Johnson story, Rachel."

"The day after Paul told me all about Benedict Arnold, we met here, like we always did, to walk to my house and listen to the program." She stopped talking, and for a minute John Alan thought she was going to cry, but she pretended she had something in her eye. He'd done that himself the past few months. "We'd met here about a million times, but I never noticed that little sign hanging down, the one that says 'B. Arnold Johnson, Proprietor.' I told Paul I bet Mr. Johnson's full name was Benedict Arnold Johnson, and that he was a dirty, rotten spy just like his great-great-great relative. You've heard about bad blood, haven't you?"

"Sure," John Alan told her. "I've heard about it,

but I never believed in it." If he believed in bad blood, he thought, then he had the very worst kind—the blood of somebody who was bad enough to leave her family.

"My father says there's no such thing, but I'm not so sure," she went on sticking her lower lip out. "I'm not so sure there's not something to the idea of bad blood. How about the Dalton gang and Jesse and Frank James? That was a bunch of *brothers* who were bank robbers, wasn't it? And then there was Ma Barker and that son of hers. Those people inherited their badness, didn't they?"

"But what about people like Simon, Rachel? People who are adopted? They got no idea what kind of blood they got. What makes people good or bad has to be in their brains, not their veins."

"Watch out! You're about to get your veins licked! Your brains, too, maybe," she laughed, pointing to Jeep, who had been waiting for her on the front porch. When he spied his new best friend, John Alan Feester, Jr., he bounded down the sidewalk like it was a hot greased griddle.

"Hey, there, Jeep!" John Alan cried, just before his arms were filled with a wiggling, barking dog again. It felt good to be loved. He'd have to explain about bad blood to Rachel some other time.

CHAPTER 18
A Lone Scout's Honor

According to what Rachel told him the next day at recess, Mrs. Dalton didn't have any trouble talking Simon's mother into letting him borrow their radio. Evidently Mrs. Green was more worried about measles and possible eye problems than she was about radios and mind pollution.

"His mother says he doesn't feel like company yet, but my mother's taking the radio over to him this afternoon," Rachel told John Alan happily. "Since we've both had the measles, he wants us to come listen to 'Captain Midnight' as soon as he feels better. That should be in about a week. We can take Jeep, too!"

"He's going to be pretty surprised that hostilities haven't broken out between us without him here to negotiate," John Alan told her.

"The week's not over, John Alan Feester," Rachel cried as the bell rang, and she raced to be first in line.

***

As they turned up the sidewalk to Simon's house the next Monday, Rachel and John Alan both spied the star flag in the window at the same time. It was exactly like the ones the Snows . . . and the Morans . . . and the Stones . . . so many families in town had in their windows, a blue star on a field of white with a red border and gold fringe around it. Still, they were surprised to see it hanging in Simon's window.

"Sure hope that star doesn't get changed to gold," Rachel whispered, kissing her finger and then pressing it against the glass in front of the star for good luck. "Hope none of them do."

"Some of 'em will, though. Some are bound to," John Alan whispered back. He turned to look at her. "You want to knock, or you want me to?"

"You go ahead. I'll try to keep Jeep from bowling Simon over. He gets crazy when he's got new rooms to smell." She grabbed the dog's collar in her fist and held on tight.

Simon and his mother were waiting in the kitchen where the only light came from a crack in the pantry door. Even after a week, he still looked like he'd fallen into a bucket of red paint. His spots had spots.

They ate their snacks while Jeep sniffed every corner of the room. When it was almost time for the program, Mrs. Green checked her watch and announced she had to run to the grocery store.

"I won't be long," she told them as she pulled on her gloves. "I'm completely out of bread. There's more cinnamon rolls and Ovaltine on the cabinet. Have fun." She dashed out the front door.

"She think she might pollute her mind if she stuck around?" John Alan teased as they took turns rubbing the fur on Jeep's head.

"Actually, she's going to the post office again. It's the third time today. To see if there's any word from my dad," Simon replied without looking up from Jeep's head. "Don't know why we pretend she's going to the store, but we do. I guess it's so when she comes home without a letter I won't be disappointed. But I always am." There was a long pause before he repeated, "I always am."

"I'm glad you mentioned your father, Simon," Rachel said, getting down on her knees next to them.

"My mother told me today about him getting shipped out. That's really awful. Wish there was something we could do."

"The worst part's the waiting," Simon sighed. "Waiting and wondering where he is. How he is. If he's ..." He chewed his thumbnail just like he used to chew that string on his silly green cap.

"Hey!" he cried, jumping up and running over to the counter the radio was on. "Want you to look at what I've figured out about the characters on the program. I wrote down their names, how they're connected to each other, and whether they're good guys or bad guys. Or in the cases of Joyce Ryan and Carla Rotan, alias Mrs. Bosmouth, good or bad girls. I love their names ... Mrs. Bosmouth! She's that, for sure. Need you to check my list. Maybe you want to check it, too, J.A., since you're as new to the program as I am."

He passed Rachel a handful of pages from a Big Chief tablet with pencil scribbling all over them. She had to move closer to the kitchen so she could read, so John Alan went with her, leaving Simon to enjoy Jeep's undivided attention.

"I haven't been able to figure out the relationship between Captain Midnight and Chuck Ramsey," Simon explained as they scanned the pages. "At first I thought Chuck was the Captain's nephew. Then I decided they were father and son, but I didn't think that worked either, since they have different last names ... although some people don't have the same last name as their father's."

"Oh, Chuck's an orphan, just like Annie," Rachel chattered as she read. "His parents died when he was a baby. Captain Midnight raised him, but he didn't want to adopt him," she blurted out before John Alan frowned at her and poked her in the ribs. Why did she have to say something like that when she knew Simon was adopted?

"I mean ... I mean ..." she stammered, "Chuck was an orphan, but he wasn't ever in an orphanage like you were, Simon, because Captain Midnight was a friend of his parents so the Captain just took him to his house when his parents died. I guess ... I guess if your real parents have friends, you don't end up ... I mean ... Oh, Simon! I have the worst motor mouth in the whole world! Just ask John Alan! I say the stupidest things sometimes! I—"

"What Rachel is trying to say," John Alan interrupted, "is that if you have relatives ... grandparents maybe, like the Snow kids did ... sometimes those relatives can take you ..." He stopped with a sigh because he wasn't doing a much better job of saying what he meant than Rachel had.

"It's okay, you two," Simon told them with a sigh. "I don't get sore when people talk about adoption ... except maybe when the teacher makes me admit in front of the whole class I don't even know when my birthday is! But Miss Cathcart didn't mean anything by that, either. She didn't know. Being an orphan and getting adopted isn't bad, though. I'm really lucky I got the parents I did. At least I know they wanted me, or they wouldn't have gone to all that trouble."

"If ... if you don't know for sure when you were born, when do you have your birthday party?" Rachel the interrogator just had to ask. John Alan had wondered the same thing himself, but he would never have asked.

"That's the best part. I get two birthdays. One's May 17. That's the day the doctor decided I was probably born by the way my belly button had healed the first time he saw me." Rachel's eyes got real big when she heard that, but it made sense to John Alan. "The other one's August 27, the day my parents took me home."

"You sure weren't there very long ... in the orphanage, I mean," Rachel murmured. "Annie was there for years."

"Annie wasn't as cute as me," Simon laughed,

cocking his head to the side. Jeep looked at him and did the same thing. Rachel tore off two pieces of her cinnamon roll and offered each of them a bite, and they all snickered, even Jeep. "Sandy, Annie's mutt, wasn't as smart as Jeep either, but they weren't real, were they?" He grinned again as he took Jeep's face in both hands and rubbed noses with him. "I remember when I was about four, a kid named Scott came to play with me. I guess he'd heard his parents say something about me being adopted, so he asked my mother if she were my *real* mother."

"What'd she say?" John Alan asked quickly. He knew for a fact some mothers were more real than others.

"She said, 'Pinch me and see! I'm as real as they come!' So Scott ran over and pinched her arm, and Mom squealed like a baby pig." He laughed again. "Hey! We're five minutes late! I can't believe I forgot to turn the radio on!"

Nobody said another word until the first commercial.

"You know the Captain went a long time thinking the Barracuda was dead," Rachel informed them while the announcer encouraged everyone, young and old alike, to drink Ovaltine for good health. "That's one thing about the program—you never know for sure who's really dead and who's just pretending to be."

"Hey, Jeep!" John Alan cried, wanting to stay as far away from the subject of people who pretended to be dead as possible. "Come here, you good old dog, you!" Simon joined them for another roll on the kitchen floor as Rachel sipped her Ovaltine and watched.

When the program was over, Simon flipped the dial and sighed.

"Sure am glad you loaned me this radio," he told Rachel, patting the top of the ivory case with both hands. "Would have been a long week if I'd just had to lie there and worry about my dad. When I can read again, it'll be lots better, but that's when my time limit on radio listening goes into effect, too."

"Time limit? You mean you get to keep listening when you're well?" Rachel squealed. "You get to listen to the Captain every day?"

"Yep ... Mom's letting me use my Christmas money from my relatives to buy my own radio! It was my dad who objected to the radio, not her. But she says he wouldn't care now. Because of the war and all. We got to keep up with what's going on. I'll have a one-hour-a-day time limit. I'm on my honor to stick to it, but that won't be hard. I'm a Lone Scout, so I know all about keeping my word."

"You're a what?" John Alan asked as he fed Jeep the last bite of his cinnamon roll. Jeep swallowed it whole, and then licked John Alan's hand for any missed crumbs.

"A Lone Scout. That's Boy Scouts for kids who don't live close enough to a town to belong to a troop. Actually, it's not around anymore, but it used to be. My dad was a Lone Scout when he was a kid, so he taught me all about it. He still has his uniform, and I wore it till it got too little. They had a real neat magazine with all the stories done by kids. He says that's how he learned to write, making up stories for the *Lone Scout* magazine."

"Is he a newspaperman like my daddy?" Rachel asked.

"He writes anything he can sell ... articles, stories, books. Mysteries, mostly. At least he did ... until he joined the navy. He worked at home so we had lots of time to do the scout stuff ... camping, hiking, singing ..." He swallowed real hard. "I hope he's still a writer. We don't know what he does. All we know is, he volunteered for the navy because he thought it was his patriotic duty." He bit his lip and looked at the blue star in the window.

"One hour a day?" John Alan broke in, changing

the subject back to the radio. "That's all you get to listen? That's not much!"

"It'll be enough for me. Captain's only fifteen minutes. I'll listen to the news the rest of the time. Mom listens to the news with me. She waits at the end of the driveway every morning for the paper, but radio news is better. Faster." He offered Rachel the last cinnamon roll. "Mom says there won't be any more cinnamon rolls for The Duration since sugar's going to be so hard to get."

"The Duration?" John Alan's ears pricked up. "What's that mean?"

"That's what everybody's calling the time between when the war started and when we win it ... The Duration. Rationing's one of a bunch of government regulations that'll last for The Duration."

"My daddy helped me work more on my rationing list," Rachel informed them, reaching in her pocket and producing a folded-up letter envelope. She flattened it out on the kitchen table. "Since paper's the first thing on my list, he says we have to use the fronts and backs of old envelopes now instead of just throwing them away. Here's what I added since the other day: paper, leather, sugar, gasoline, aluminum, silk, nylon, butter, tin, and coffee. There's going to be lots more things rationed till The

Duration's over!" She looked at John Alan as she added, "I already knew what The Duration meant before Simon told you!"

"If your daddy's so smart, he should've told you to add teachers to that list of yours," John Alan snapped, matching her uppityness with some of his own.

"Teachers! They couldn't ration teachers!" Rachel replied, stamping her foot and causing Jeep to start whining. "That's a stupid thing to say."

"It is *not* stupid!" John Alan replied, hands on his hips now. "Your father may have a Teletype and know about things like the Rose Bowl being moved, Rachel Dalton, but my father knows about schools. He told me there are teacher shortages on both coasts already. His friend in California told him about it when they talked long distance last week! Men are being drafted and the women are going to work in factories."

"But you can't ration people like you ration a sack of sugar! How'll they do that, Mr. Know-It-All Feester? Tell me that, huh? Huh?"

"Wait a minute! Wait a minute!" Simon said, stepping between them. "J.A.! Rachel! You all remind me of those incendiary bombs they're always showing in the newsreels at the picture show. What happened to your truce?"

"Truce!" Rachel muttered. "What truce? John Alan Feester is a leopard who can't change his spots, that's all he is! And a big fat enigma to boot!" Rachel pulled on her coat and gloves, grabbed Jeep by the collar, and headed toward the door. The dog started howling and trying to get back to John Alan, but Rachel was determined to leave and take Jeep with her.

"Aw, Rachel, you promised me I could race him home!" he pleaded, but she scooped the dog up in her arms and told Simon to open the door for her.

"I'd rather be dead than red in the head!" John Alan hollered before Simon could get the door closed. Simon shook his head and poured himself another glass of Ovaltine.

CHAPTER 19
The Truth, At Last

Simon negotiated another truce, a longer-lasting one this time because so much happened in January that Rachel and John Alan didn't have time to fight.

Rachel received her first letter from Paul, and Miss Cathcart asked her to read it to the class so they'd be inspired to make his birthday banner. The letter told all about his trip to California, and Miss Cathcart really bragged on his writing ability. But since Paul hadn't even asked Rachel to tell him hello, John Alan didn't think it was such a hot letter. He'd kept Paul's secret, hadn't he? He could have at least asked her to tell him "hi." John Alan helped make the birthday banner, but he didn't sign his name like everybody else did.

The day Paul's second letter came, John Alan and Rachel happened to be in the post office at the same time. He watched as she pulled the letter out of the box, but since she just stuck it in her pocket and ran out the door, he didn't ask her about it when he ended up behind her in line the next morning before school. Maybe Paul said something bad about him this time, and she wouldn't want to show him the letter.

"If you and Simon will meet me at Daddy Warbucks' at recess, I'll let you read Paul's letter," she said, turning around and walking backwards as the line started toward the door.

"Sure. Sure thing," John Alan replied, sighing a big sigh of relief. "I'll tell Simon when we get inside."

When he got to the room, John Alan discovered Simon was home sick with a cold. His mother had called Miss Cathcart and asked her to have John Alan drop his homework off on his way home. John Alan was secretly glad it would be just the two of them, but he didn't tell Rachel that as they walked toward the trees. He didn't want her to know he was really starting to like her.

"It's got a return address this time," she told him, carefully pulling the letter from its envelope so she wouldn't tear anything. "I've read it about ten times already, and since it doesn't have any military secrets in it, I didn't have to censor it." She lowered her voice. "They censor Uncle Otis and Uncle Claude's letters." She handed him the letter. "I know Paul won't care if you read this. He's having an awful time, and ... and ... I thought maybe if I let you read this you might ... you might write him a letter back. I know he'd like that."

"You think Paul would like to get a letter from *me?*" John Alan blurted out. "Paul hates my guts!"

"Paul never hated anybody's guts in his life, John Alan. And I know for a fact that he likes you. He told me so. In writing."

"When in writing? He sure never mentioned me in that first letter you got," John Alan said as he picked up a rock and began to drop it back and forth in his hands like it was a baseball.

"Well ... well ... that letter I read to the class wasn't the first letter I got from Paul." She began to talk so fast and so softly John Alan had a hard time keeping up with her. "The first one ... the letter where he told me he stole my pencil box and that you saw him do it—"

"Loose lips sink ships!" John Alan broke in when he realized what she was telling him. She knew!

Rachel knew the truth about the pencil box! He stopped dropping the rock and stared at her.

"What was that you said about lips and ships?" she wanted to know.

"Loose lips sink ships," John Alan repeated. "That's what it says on the new navy poster. I helped Miss Peevehouse put it up on the bulletin board in the library yesterday. It means the same thing as Miss Cathcart's 'Don't tell everything you know.'" He looked her straight in the eyes. "I've never told everything I knew, Rachel. Never."

"Well, I'm not telling everything now either," Rachel said, looking at Paul's letter in John Alan's hand, "but I will tell you this much. Paul told me the whole story ... that he took my pencil box and why he did it, that you and Kenneth saw him but didn't tell, that he thought he was having to move because he'd been a traitor to me, and that I should try to be friends with you. Then he said he was sure you weren't all bad and that he was going to miss you."

"He said that? He said all that?"

"He did. And I'm sorry I waited so long to tell you. But ... but ... well, you read this letter now, and maybe ... maybe someday I'll let you read the other one, the letter he left with my pencil box." She handed him the letter. "Would you read it out loud?

That would kind of make me feel like Paul was talking to me."

John Alan had to clear his throat three times before he could begin the letter, which read:

Dear Rachely Nachely,

Remember how Grandpa Griggs used to call you that when we were little kids? He even made up a poem about you, but all I can remember of it is the line "you come by it nachely." I can remember almost everything else we ever said or did, though. In fact, I spend more time remembering Oklahoma than I do thinking about what's going on now because what's going on now is not much fun. I sure miss you and Oklahoma. And Kenneth and John Alan, too. I hope they'll write to me.

Can't remember when I sent you that first letter, but I'm writing this on January 17.

John Alan stopped to figure a minute. The letter had taken about a week to get there. He'd wondered how long letters from California took. Not that his mother would ever write him one. But she did send him that angel, didn't she? With the war, Simon's measles, and Rachel's resistance to think about, he hadn't had as much time to worry about his mother ... about Toad ... as he used to. But she was still wiggling around down in that secret sack. He went back to reading Paul's letter.

Anyway, we finally found a dinky little room to rent, but we have to share it with a man we don't even know. That's what everybody out here has to do. The man (his name is John Wilson) works the day shift, and so does Pop, so he and Pop sleep on the two army cots while Mom works the night shift. They don't allow kids in this building, so I have to sneak in after the landlady goes to sleep. She plays the piano till her bedtime, so I wait until I don't hear it tinkling anymore and then I slip in. I have to be real careful not to wake Pop or Mr. Wilson or they get real mad. I sleep on the floor. The room is just big enough for the two cots, a little table with two stools, and a hot plate instead of a stove. I never ate so much soup in my life! Sure wish I had some of your mom's home cooking. Tell her that, okay? And tell your father and Al I said "Hi!" too.

I started school last Wednesday, so I have a place to be most of the time while Mom sleeps. You're going to find this hard to believe, but I'm the only white kid in the class and none of the other kids are Indians! Everybody else is Japanese, Chinese, or Mexican. Isn't that amazing? Not one Indian! Weren't at least a third of the kids in our class Indians? I never counted, but I think that's about right. Anyway, the two I like best so far are Japanese, which is kind of funny since they are supposed to be our enemy. But these two guys, Max and Woody, were both born here in El Centro. Their parents were born in California, too. Some of the new kids (there are lots of us) try to give them a hard time, but our teacher is Japanese, too, and she's been teaching about a hundred years so she knows how to keep law and order. (She's not mean like Odious Oxley, though.) Her name is Miss Lee and she was born in California, too. I really do like her.

Everything is so crowded here you can't go anywhere without almost getting trampled. The cars don't watch where they're going, and everybody looks like they're lost all the time. I've only met one other kid in school from Oklahoma so far. She's in the sixth grade. She told me she and her little brothers sleep in the back of the closet every night because they're so scared.

Her parents both work the eleven to seven

shift, so she has to watch her little brothers. They live in a cabin in a tourist court. It's about the size of that playhouse Shirley Jean had, remember? It was mighty crowded in there if we had more than two kids. Well, this girl, Kay is her name, lives there all the time with her mother and father and twin brothers who are six. WOW! And I don't mean Words of Wisdom!

I haven't been able to listen to Captain Midnight even once since I left Oklahoma, so write me a long letter and tell me everything that's happened. The one good thing is I get to go to lots of picture shows. I saw *Goodbye, Mr. Chips, Sergeant York,* and *Grapes of Wrath* this week. I liked the first two, but *Grapes of Wrath* was awful because it made everybody in Oklahoma look real, real dumb and the kids at school teased me about it.

I've learned how to stand up on the toilet stool in the bathroom in the picture show between pictures so they can't see my feet and make me go back outside and pay again. All that stuff Captain Midnight taught us about sneaking and spying is paying off at last. Ha! Ha!

The first week, Mom cried a lot and begged Pop to let me and her get on a bus and come home, but that just made him mad and you know when he's mad he drinks a lot and ... Oh, well. Anyway, she's stopped crying now. At least when I'm around. I don't know when they're going to start making all that money Pop talks about all the time, but I hope it's soon. Everything here is real expensive.

Well, I better close for now or this letter is going to need extra postage, and we're really short of cash right now. Mom and Pop haven't got paid yet because there was a mix-up in their paper work. Pop says they'll have it figured out by the end of the week. Then we'll be wading in high cotton. I think that means we'll be doing real well.

Please write me back the day you get this. I need to know everything that's going on back there. Are you still resisting John Alan? Is he still offering you aid and comfort? I hope not. I sure do miss you, Rachel.

Yours truly,
Paul

When John Alan looked up, he saw tears in Rachel's eyes, and he almost got some in his, but he was better than she was at swallowing tears. He folded the letter up just as carefully as she had unfolded it, put it back in the envelope, and handed it to her.

"Thanks for letting me read it. Thanks a lot. I'll write him. I'll tell him we're friends now," he told her.

"I'm glad Simon was sick today," she said, throwing her head back and looking at the topmost branch of the tallest tree just like John Alan had done when he asked her about his mother. "I mean, I wouldn't have wanted to tell you all those things about Paul and my pencil box if Simon had been here. He ... he wasn't around Paul enough to know ... to know Paul could never be a traitor to anybody. Or a thief either. Not really."

"I know," John Alan told her. "I know there are some secrets you can never tell. I know all there is to know about keeping secrets, Rachely Nachely." He gave her a lopsided grin before he added, "And I'm really really sorry Paul's having such a bad time."

She held the letter over her heart as she whispered, "I am, too, J.A. I am, too."

CHAPTER 20
Enter Odious Oxley

The first Monday of the second semester brought even more changes. On that day, Simon was able to convince John Alan and Rachel to extend their truce for The Duration. He was able to accomplish this amazing feat because of a most unlikely ally: Miss Sadie Oxley.

They started to feel very uneasy when, in spite of the fact it was a very cold day, no fifth-grade students were allowed in the building before school, not even to use the bathroom. They huddled together against the January cold and watched a parade of high school boys walk back and forth from the north door of the grade school to the old bus barn carrying desks.

When the bell finally rang, and the students in 5B began to march into the building, the news was rapidly whispered back down the line that it was Miss Oxley who stood behind the teacher's desk in their room instead of Miss Cathcart. Miss Odious Oxley.

"I bet Miss Cathcart finally got the measles," Rachel whispered into John Alan's ear when the news reached her at the end of the line. "Wish it had been Odious Oxley instead!" They were standing a long way from where the line curved around the corner of the door and at least fifty feet from Miss Oxley.

"I heard that, Rachel Elizabeth Dalton," Miss Oxley bellowed in a voice that reminded John Alan of a cement mixer—loud, rough, and gravelly. "I would caution you to keep your opinions and comments to yourself if you do not wish to be held accountable!"

John Alan whipped around in time to watch Rachel's mouth drop open. He put his hand under her chin and pushed her jaws closed. Then he put his finger to his own lips in a shush symbol like the sailor in that navy poster he'd shown her in the library. He wanted to whisper, "Loose lips sink ships!" but he didn't dare. Unless Miss Oxley's sight was even more powerful than her hearing (the woman might be able see around corners!), she wouldn't know he'd given Rachel a little real "aid and comfort." But Rachel knew, and she gave him a weak smile as she flashed a V for victory.

"Take your seats immediately!" Miss Oxley commanded. "Lack of attention will bring you detention!" She was notorious for her silly jingles and for keeping more students in after-school detention than any teacher in the history of the school. As they marched in lockstep toward their seats, John Alan, Rachel, and Simon took turns sliding their eyes back and forth between each other and the ogre behind Miss Cathcart's desk. Miss Oxley waited until everyone was seated before she spoke again.

"It is my duty to inform you that Miss Mae Ella Cathcart has chosen to answer her country's call and take a job in a defense plant." She cleared her throat and waited for her announcement to sink in. "We admire her courage and determination. However, due to the critical shortage of qualified teachers, her departure will necessitate the combining of 5A and 5B into one class for the rest of the year if not for The Duration."

The Duration! A collective groan rolled over the room like thunder across an Oklahoma prairie, deepening the wrinkles in Miss Oxley's forehead. She glared at each child in turn, but she focused on Rachel longer than on anybody else. John Alan winced as he watched Rachel's face turn bright red. He used to enjoy watching that happen, but not anymore.

"Mr. Feester, Sr.," Miss Oxley said, without so much as a glance toward John Alan (she didn't give a fig who his father was) "is in the process of moving 5A to what was once the bus barn but is now our classroom." Everybody groaned again. That barn was the cold and drafty metal building where they had recess when the weather was bad outside. They couldn't have school there! They'd all freeze to death!

"I will not tolerate moans and groans from namby-pamby boys and girls who do not know the meaning of the word *sacrifice!*" Miss Oxley told them in a slow and measured tone. "Our country is at war, and sacrifices are being made every day far greater than those you are being called upon to accept."

She waited a moment before she went on, but when she did, her tone was just as hard. "There will be forty students in this combined class, which will present a challenge to me, as your teacher, as well as to each of you. I am ready and willing to accept that challenge, and I expect you to give me your full cooperation. Talking in class will be kept to a minimum, and failure to raise one's hand and be recognized will result in a one-hour detention."

Once again she allowed her eyes to travel up and

down each row in the room, pausing to stare into each face. John Alan thought she looked like she was memorizing their features so she could pick them out of a police lineup if she ever had to call the cops.

"Mr. Schwartz has provided sturdy grocery sacks for you to put your books and supplies in for the move, and I will pass those out in a moment. Since paper is now in short supply, you must handle the sacks with care. When we have finished the move, we will place them in our wagons for next week's paper drive. The high school students who moved 5A's desks have already filled one of my wagons. They will come for your desks when we have completed our opening exercises."

She stalked out from behind Miss Cathcart's desk, stood in front of the flag, and ordered, "All rise for the Pledge of Allegiance and the singing of our National Anthem!"

John Alan Feester, Jr., slid out of his desk along with everybody else in his class and stood at attention. He placed his hand on his heart and, for the first time ever, was very aware that the rest of the class was touching their hearts, too. This war, which only two months ago seemed such a long way away, had just marched into all of their lives. For The Duration.

CHAPTER 21
Truce for "The Duration"

The move was completed by noon because no one involved was allowed a morning recess. That added to the cloud of gloom that quickly formed over the cold bus barn classroom and its new occupants. Desks were aligned in perfectly straight rows, bookcases were assembled and filled with dictionaries, encyclopedias, and other reference books. The flags of Oklahoma and the United States were standing in their proper places on either side of Miss Oxley's desk, and President Franklin D. Roosevelt's picture was hung on the wall over the free-standing blackboard. All by 11:45.

Lunch sacks were provided to those who had

thought they were going home to eat, and those who had brought theirs to begin with joined them for a twenty-minute lunch break. To make the morning news an even more bitter pill to swallow, they learned that their parents had been informed of Miss Cathcart's departure over the weekend. At Miss Oxely's request, they had not told their children. When the students learned that, they ate their lunches in total silence. After lunch, Miss Oxley continued to bark commands until she was forced to free them for afternoon recess.

They scattered like a herd of wild mustangs that discovered an opening in the stockade fence.

"How come you didn't warn us Miss Cathcart was leaving, John Alan? Surely *you* knew," Rachel quizzed him when she finally caught her breath. In spite of the cold, she, John Alan, and Simon were hunkered down in Daddy Warbucks' mansion trying to figure out how they were going to endure the rest of the year.

"Remember what I told you about my family and secrets?" he grumbled, blowing hard into his cupped hands to warm them. He'd misplaced his gloves in the move, but he wasn't about to report it to Odious Oxley. He'd let his fingers freeze off before he did that. "My father's the heavyweight champion of the secret-keeping world."

It was true. His father never discussed important matters with him—or with his mother either. He had wondered if that was one of the reasons she left. He wished he could ask her. Funny how other bad stuff happening to him, like Miss Cathcart leaving, made him think about Toad again. It wasn't that he'd forgotten, but having friends to hang around with, having Rachel let him read her letters, having Simon call him J.A.—things like that had made life easier for him somehow.

"Wouldn't have done any good if we'd known," Simon told them with a shrug. "We couldn't have done anything about it. We're just kids, and kids can't change much. I begged my father not to join the navy, not to go away and leave us. To wait and take his luck with the draft. But he said he couldn't live with himself if he let other men defend his family, so I gave up. I'm proud of him, but ... but ... that doesn't ... that doesn't ..." He bit his lip and stared off into space.

"Wonder where she's going?" Rachel mused, wanting to change the subject. "Bet it's to be somewhere near Joe Bob Snow." She'd told them a million times about Miss Cathcart being sweet on Joe Bob, that she knew for a fact they'd been together at the New Year's Dance at the Legion Hall, that Miss Cathcart had gone to the bus station to see him off when he left New Year's Day. She'd told them all of that.

But she didn't know about that can of dirt! Even though her own big brother had been there when it happened, she didn't know about the can of dirt from Mrs. Snow's garden. John Alan was certain of that. If she'd known, she'd have told that, too. Rachel and her big mouth. He felt the old urge to shut her up stirring in his bones.

"She couldn't follow Joe Bob, Rachel," he scoffed. "Nobody knew where he was being shipped. He didn't even know himself. You're pretty dumb to say—"

"My dad didn't know either," Simon interrupted him. "Everything is a military secret now. Remember, 'Loose lips sink ships!' And if you two don't learn to button yours ... lips, that is ... both of you are going to be spending the rest of your lives in detention." He pointed toward the cold bus barn, now ruled by Miss Sadie Oxley. "She's not going to allow resistance of any kind, not against her, or against each other either. You don't have any choice, Rachel and J.A. You've got to call a truce for The Duration!"

"For The Duration?" they repeated at the same time.

"For The Duration! Cross your hearts and hope to die!" Simon commanded. He'd never made them do that before. They looked at each other and then at the cold bus barn just as Miss Oxley stepped out of the door and whistled. She didn't even have a real whistle; she just pinched her lower lip together with her fingers and made the loudest, shrillest sound they'd ever heard in their lives.

"Truce for The Duration," they pledged. "Cross our hearts and hope to die." They quickly slashed across their chests as they jumped up and started to run for the building.

"Stop and shake on it!" Simon commanded.

"But we're gonna be—"

"Stop and shake!"

They stopped.

They shook.

And then they ran.

And Rachel's resistance was put on hold for The Duration.

CHAPTER 22
Miss Oxley's Secret Squadron

"Today we are going to discuss one of the many threats to our war efforts," Miss Oxley began class the next morning. "Who can tell us what the infinitive 'to hoard' means?"

Rachel clamped one hand over her mouth and shot the other in the air. Simon had made her practice doing that during the whole "Captain Midnight" program the day before.

"It's the only way you're going to keep out of detention," he'd warned her. "You got to learn to raise your hand before you open your mouth. It's got to become a conditioned reflex . . . that's where you train one part of your body to react to another part of your body. Miss Cathcart allowed you to blurt out questions and answers all the time, but those days are over!" Every time Captain or Joyce or anybody else on the program asked a question, Rachel had to pretend she wanted to answer it and raise her hand. If she forgot, Simon wrote her name down under the word *Detention* on a sheet of paper, while John Alan laughed his head off. Simon was a hard taskmaster, but he was effective. He now gave Rachel a big grin and a thumbs-up sign for remembering.

John Alan saw a little smile playing around the edges of Miss Oxley's lips as she noted the hand over Rachel's mouth, but the smile slipped away before she called on her. Odious Oxley might not be all bad, he decided when he saw that smile. Nobody's all bad.

"Rachel, you may answer," Miss Oxley ordered. "Stand and speak clearly. This is a large and cavernous room."

"To hoard means to buy up a whole bunch of hard-to-find stuff like automobile tires or nylon stockings and hide them so you and your family are the only ones who have them. People are starting to hoard everything that's about to be rationed—even food!"

"You are correct, Rachel. You may sit down. Hoarding," she went on, "as I said earlier, is becoming a great threat to our war effort. Our government is depending on each and every one of us to deny ourselves for the common good. Only people who are as un-American and un-patriotic as Ivan Shark and The Barracuda would hoard at a time like this."

"Did you say Ivan Shark!" Rachel blurted out and then watched as Miss Oxley wrote her name under *Detention* on the right-hand side of the board.

"Report immediately after school, Rachel," Miss Oxley ordered before she turned to the blackboard and wrote *hoard* under *Words of War,* which she had printed in red in the left-hand corner of the board.

John Alan was as stunned as Rachel and the other thirty-eight kids in Miss Sadie Oxley's newly formed fifth-grade class. Odious Oxley had just named Captain Midnight's two worst enemies as people who would hoard. Odious Oxley listened to the program! John Alan just knew she couldn't be as bad as everybody said. Nobody was all bad. He was sorry about Rachel's detention, but rules were rules.

"'Use it up, wear it out, make it do, or do without!' That's the motto Captain Midnight himself repeated at the end of the program last Friday," Miss Oxley went on. "I couldn't have done better myself!

Soon you will see those words on posters all across America. They will be our class motto. 'Use it up, wear it out, make it do, or do without!' Now, take out your spelling notebooks, and turn to this week's list."

There was a rustling and shuffling of papers as they did as they were told. Eighty hands make a lot of noise, even when they're trying not to. Miss Oxley frowned, but she didn't shush them.

"In addition to the twenty words listed each week, we will add five more having to do with the war and the war effort."

There was a collective groan. Twenty-five words! That was against the rules of the Geneva Convention!

"I will caution you," she said, narrowing her eyes, "I have been known to keep entire classrooms in detention on the same day. Another groan from this group, and you will find yourselves in that category. Add the following words to your spelling list for this week."

She turned and wrote *nylon, glycerin, grenades,* and *afghan* on the blackboard under *hoard.* "You are all familiar with nylon because of the stockings your mothers wear. You also know that those stockings are in very short supply since nylon is now going into items like parachutes and towropes for glider planes." Shirley Jean shot her hand into the air. "Yes, Shirley Jean? You have a question?"

"My grandpa has a store, and he gets nylons once in a while, and when he does, he mails them straight to my Uncle Jack so he can trade them for things he needs. Uncle Jack's in the army, and he says where he's stationed, those girls will do anything for a pair of nylon hose!"

"Well ... well, yes ..." Miss Oxley stammered. "Moving right along ... The next word, *glycerin,* might not be as familiar to you. We are all being asked to save waste fat—frying fat and bacon drippings—because the fat is manufactured into powder used to make bullets. You know what hand grenades are, but you probably do not know our school is getting ready to donate all our old radiators to the war effort because they contain iron, which can be made into hand grenades." Jean Margaret's hand went up this time. "A question, Jean Margaret?"

"My grandma's knitting that next word for the Red Cross!" she stated proudly. "I can't ever say it right, but I know how to spell it. It sounds kind of like the name of people from a country a long way from here."

"It does, indeed, Jean Margaret. That's because it's the same word. When the word *Afghan* is written with a capital letter, it means people from Afghanistan, a country in Asia. With a small letter, it's a knitted shawl or blanket. I picked it for this week's list because our class is going to be knitting afghan squares for the Red Cross."

"Even the boys?" John Alan spat out before he even knew he said it.

"Right after school, John Alan," she said as she added his name to Rachel's. "And yes, even the boys in this class will learn to knit afghans. If we are to win this war, gender differences are going to have to be forgotten. More and more women are doing men's jobs in factories all over the United States now. It's certainly not going to hurt the boys of Theodore Roosevelt Elementary School to learn to knit!"

CHAPTER 23
Changes, Changes, Changes

In spite of the almost daily changes in their lives, John Alan and the other students in Miss Oxley's class began to settle into as much of a routine as is possible when the whole world is at war. Odious Oxley ruled the class with an iron fist, but the fact that she was a "Captain Midnight" fan kept them all looking for the good that John Alan said was in every human being, even Miss Oxley. After all, he'd changed his ways, hadn't he?

He even gave in and learned to knit when the Red Cross lady came and told them how important it was for the war effort. He wasn't as good at it as Rachel and Simon, but it was so cold in the bus barn, they were all glad to be able to hold the warm wool in their hands, even for a little while.

As February approached, they looked forward to Groundhog Day so Punxsutawney Phil could tell them whether or not there would be six more weeks of winter. They sure hoped not. Not in that barn. They even got Miss Oxley to agree that if Phil didn't see his shadow on February 2, they could have a small, quiet party during the noon hour. Nothing big—just a few games at their seats.

But once again, the war stepped in. Phil was not allowed to predict the weather in the United States for fear the enemy might use that knowledge to its advantage.

"Another record broken!" Simon lamented at recess the day they heard the bad news. "Phil's been predicting the weather since 1886, and now his show's been canceled! I can't believe it!" He yanked his silly green hat off and threw it on the ground.

"Good grief, Simon, was that in those encyclopedias of yours?" Rachel asked as she picked up his cap and pulled it back down on his head. She stopped short of tying it under his chin because the strings were always wet where he chewed on them.

"I'm from Pennsylvania, remember? I've seen Phil in person! We drove over to Punxsutawney three different years to watch him creep out of that hole. My dad really did ... really does ... love that groundhog." It had been so long since they'd heard from his father, Simon had a hard time knowing whether to use the past or present tense. John Alan had the same problem, but since he never talked about his mother out loud, his problem was only in his head.

"First the Rose Bowl game gets moved, then we go on War Time, now they're canceling Groundhog Day," John Alan moaned. "What's next?"

What was next was Valentine's Day. Since both red and white paper were in short supply, what they could find was cut into hearts to send to the many boys in the service whose pictures now crowded the bulletin board in the library. Miss Peevehouse barely got Jack Snow's picture up in time because he left just the week before, but he got a heart, too.

Rachel, of course, remembered to mail Paul's birthday banner, which Miss Cathcart had entrusted to her.

"It sure seems silly now," she told Simon and John Alan, who had gone with her to the post office, "but Paul's and my Friday the thirteenth Good Luck birthdays seemed like the most important events in the world not very long ago. Never thought he'd be in California when his birthday came, and I wouldn't even want to have a party at all. Kind of makes you think there might be something to triskaidekaphobia, doesn't it?"

Ten days after Paul's birthday, a Japanese submarine surfaced off Goleta, California, and shelled an oil refinery. It happened while President Roosevelt was making one of his "fireside chats." It didn't do much damage and nobody was killed, but it brought the war right to the soil of one of the forty-eight states. Air raid drills were ordered all across the country.

When he crawled in bed each night, John Alan thought of that dirt from Mrs. Snow's garden, and he began to wonder if maybe those Friday the thirteenths in February and March were the cause of America's bad luck in the war. He didn't blame Rachel for deciding not to have a birthday party this year. It didn't seem right to celebrate these days. Not when America was losing battle after battle in far-away places with strange-sounding names like the Java Sea and Sunda Strait.

He got out of bed and went to the closet to check on his angel more and more often. She was still there and still trying to get that pass off, but he knew there was nobody downfield to catch it if she did. He never took her out of the box. He just looked at her and then closed the lid.

"It's still a dumb present," he told the darkness that filled his room, "not good for anything."

CHAPTER 24
The Worst News Yet

Rachel was positive Paul would send her a birthday card. He had drawn and colored her a fancy one every year since they were three, she told John Alan and Simon many times. She still had every one of them. He'd told them in a letter how much he liked his birthday banner, how he had taken it to school to show everybody, how Miss Lee had said he must have lots and lots of good friends in Oklahoma. He wanted to hang it in the little room where they lived, but his father wouldn't let him.

When he found out about the truce, and when Simon and John Alan both started writing him, too, Paul began to send just one letter a week to the three of them to save money and paper. He took turns with the names on the envelopes. Rachel didn't mind that, but she knew that her birthday card, her eleventh birthday card, would be addressed to her and nobody else. He would mail it early so it would arrive in time. Paul always did everything on time. But her birthday came, and there was no card.

There was, however, a letter.

It was addressed to John Alan since it was his turn, but he handed it to Rachel so she could read it first. She handed it back to him.

"You read it to Simon and me, John Alan. This is Friday the thirteenth, and I've got an awful feeling this is gonna be bad news. I just know it is. I hope Paul's father didn't run off and leave them way out there with no money or no way to get home."

John Alan led them over to a corner in the post office and began to read the letter.

Dear Rachel, John Alan, and Simon,

This is going to be a real hard letter to write, but I got to get this story out of my head or it's going to pop my brain open like that watermelon we dropped out of your upstairs window last year, Rachel. Remember that? I thought looking down at that smashed-to-smithereens watermelon, and

175

at Miss Peevehouse in her ruined dress, was the worst thing I'd ever seen my life. But it was nothing compared to what I saw yesterday.

My two friends, Max and Woody, got taken to prison. So did our teacher, Miss Lee. So were all the other Japanese people in town. Here's what happened.

About a week ago, all the Japanese people around here . . . even the kids . . . got told they were going to have to move, and they just had one week to get ready! Nobody would tell them why, nobody would tell them where they were moving to. Nobody would tell them nothing except to pack what they could stuff in boxes and suitcases! They didn't even get to take their furniture. They didn't even get to take their toys or books!

The first day they got told, everybody still came to school. Miss Lee led us in the Pledge of Allegiance and The Star Spangled Banner like always but half of the class was crying their eyes out while they said it and sang it because it's Americans that's making them move and they are Americans themselves.

That happened last week and every day since less and less of the Japanese kids showed up for school. Max and Woody haven't been here in three days. I went by their apartments and tried to talk to them, but both of them told me to go away, that I was nothing but a dumb Okie and they never wanted to see me again. It was awful, but I couldn't get them to even let me in to talk to them.

Then yesterday it happened. About a zillion cattle trucks rolled down the street. They made an awful racket, so everybody in every apartment was hanging out the widows to see what was going on. Those trucks stopped in front of the buildings and soldiers in uniforms carrying guns rounded up every Japanese person they could find and loaded them in the trucks. Cattle trucks! Even the grownups were crying and hollering, and everybody was looking for their kids because there was such a mob that lots of families got lost from each other. It was so terrible I can't even write about it without bawling my eyes out.

Those trucks didn't even turn off their engines and the exhaust from all those motors was awful. I tried to find Max and Woody so I could tell them good-bye and how sorry I was, but I didn't see them or anybody in their families so I finally came on home.

I still don't know what's going on because we don't have a radio and I can't buy newspapers cause we don't have any extra money. Mr. Wilson said he heard that all the Japanese in California are being taken to prison camps way out in the desert. Somebody else said they were going to have to live in horse stalls out at the racetrack, but I'm sure that's not true. Mr. Wilson says they deserve whatever happens to them because of Pearl Harbor. He says they all need to be locked away because they all got bad blood.

John Alan stopped reading for a minute and looked up at Simon, but he couldn't tell by the look on Simon's face how he felt about what Paul had just said. He started reading again, faster this time.

But I know that's not true because Max and Woody are Americans even if they are Japanese. They're sure not like the ones who bombed Pearl Harbor. Max has a big brother in the U.S. Navy and Woody does, too, so their blood must be American! Woody's real name is Woodrow after President Woodrow Wilson! His parents named him that, so it's crazy to say he's got bad blood!

John Alan stopped reading and looked up at Simon again. He couldn't read those words again and not say *something*. He didn't want Simon to feel as bad as Paul.

"Paul's right about that, Simon," Rachel said softly. "Being a good or bad person doesn't have anything to do with your blood. I know that now for sure."

"Only bad blood I ever knowed of wuz that 'tween them Hatfields and them McCoys," Simon drawled in a great imitation of the actor Walter Brennan. He hitched his fingers through imaginary overall straps as he added, "Them families shed a whole bucket of bad blood in their time." Simon always had a way of making them smile, even in the worst of times. Then he got serious again. "Go on, John Alan, finish the letter."

The end of the letter went like this:

Well, I feel a little better now that I've told you what happened, but not much. Maybe your father could find out what's going on and tell you and then you could tell me about it. My parents don't tell me much of anything.

Write me again soon. I sure do miss all of you. Simon, you sure do talk more on paper than you did in person! HA! HA!

Paul

P.S. I don't know when we're going wading in that "high cotton" my father is always talking about. He's still spending all our money on horses and beer.

P.P.S. I'm sorry I didn't draw you a birthday card this year, but I don't even have any crayons or paper out here! I'm beginning to think there's something to that triskaidekaphobia stuff! The only good thing about my birthday was my banner, and it came on the 12th not the 13th!

Rachel folded up the letter and held it tight in both hands.

"This can't be true," Rachel told them, stomping her foot. "Paul has to be mistaken. This letter's real old. I bet it's all straightened out by now. American soldiers wouldn't take other Americans and lock them up like that when they hadn't done anything. That just can't be true. Why haven't we heard about it?"

"Well, for one thing, because there aren't any Japanese in Apache. For another, we're kids, and none of the adults I know talk about bad stuff when we're around," Simon reminded her. "Our own parents didn't even tell us Miss Cathcart was leaving till she was gone!"

"Well, I'm gonna go ask my father! Come on, go

with me!" Rachel shouted. They raced each other out the door and down the street.

***

"Well, kids, you see it's a pretty hush-hush business from what I've heard so far," Mr. Dalton told them after he'd read Paul's letter. "But President Roosevelt himself gave the okay for the detention camps, so he must have his reasons. Don't know if they are good ones or not though. Remember," he said with a sad smile, "he's a Democrat!"

"Detention camps? They call them detention camps instead of prisons? Detention is when you have to stay after school for talking too much, Daddy. It's not getting locked up! It's not fair to do that to innocent people! It's not fair at all!"

"War's never fair, Punkin. War causes people to do terrible things. I told you that the day Pearl Harbor got bombed and that brick got thrown through Sam Sing's laundry window. And all because someone didn't like the shape of his eyes. I told you it was going to get a lot worse, but this is one time I'm really sorry I was right."

"There ought to be something we can do!"

"There are ways you kids can help ... collect paper, collect tin, knit afghans ... I hear you've got a real fast pair of needles, John Alan!" he teased. "You can keep writing Paul and trying to cheer him up. Losing friends is hard to take. You know that, Rachel. But you got new ones," he pointed at Simon and John Alan. "Paul will, too."

He looked at the letter again. "Besides all the other sadness in this, you have to really feel for those military boys, the sons of those poor people. Be pretty hard to serve your country if you knew your own family had been locked up by your very own government. It's hard enough on people like the Snows, but at least they're waiting things out in their own home. I saw Mrs. Snow out working in her garden when I came to work today. She says she's not planting any new flowers this year. It's going to be a fruit and vegetable victory garden like everybody else has these days. Still, I bet it'll be the prettiest place in town come June."

When June arrived, no flowers appeared at the Snows' house.

But a telegram did.

CHAPTER 25
Joe Bob's Angel

"Go away! I don't want to see nobody!" John Alan heard Mrs. Snow cry out when he knocked at the back door of their house. It had been two weeks since the "killed in action" telegram had been delivered. He had sneaked down the alley and up to the back door so he wouldn't have to pass that flag with two blue stars hanging in the front window. One blue star needed to be changed to gold now. "You go on away! I talked to all the people I ever want to talk to. I don't need no more newspapermen sticking their noses in my private business!"

"Please, Mrs. Snow," he pleaded. "I'm not a newspaperman. It's just me, John Alan Feester."

"Go away, I say! Go away!"

"My ... my ... father's John Alan Feester, Sr., ... the superintendent of schools ... remember him?" he hollered. He hated himself for saying that because he knew that now she'd have to let him in. His father was her husband's boss. But John Alan needed to see her, wanted to see her real bad, and telling her who his father was seemed to be his only chance. So he said it.

The door swung open very slowly, its hinges squeaking like the handle on his grandmother's old cistern when he went outside to draw water for her. He wished his grandmother were here with him now. He wished somebody was. He couldn't ask Rachel or Simon because he didn't want them to know what he was doing. They'd ask too many questions. He stood in the doorway and waited for her to ask him in.

"There's been a mistake. You know that, don't you, John Alan Feester, Jr.?" she told him, her head bobbing up and down sideways like a puppet with a broken string. "He just got lost, you know? They lost track of where he was, that's all. He's not ... he's not ... dead! Joe Bob ain't been in the war long enough to die!"

She motioned him in and began to wail as John Alan crept into her tiny kitchen. He had thought the same thing when he heard the news from Rachel. Joe Bob hadn't been in battle long enough to get killed. How long did it take? How long was long enough?

"I . . . I brought you something," he told her, holding out the cigar-sized box which now had the silver paper taped back on it. He wished it had a ribbon. The kitchen felt cold, even though it was a hot day in June. All the burners on the gas cookstove had been lit and turned up as high as they would go. Mrs. Snow still had a box of matches clutched in her hand, and he could see she had burned her fingers lighting those burners. They were red and starting to blister, but she didn't seem to feel it.

"For me?" she said, putting her hand to her mouth and drawing back as if the box were a live hand grenade. "I don't want no present." She put the box of matches down and began to back away. "Thank you kindly, young Mr. Feester, but I don't want no present."

A half-grown pup slunk into the room and began to circle the table, whining and howling like he'd just been run over by Joe Hoskin's coal truck. He looked just like Jeep.

"That poor dog! That poor little pup!" Mrs. Snow

moaned over and over again. "That hound knowed. He knowed the minute the knock came on that door. He knowed before I opened it and seen Tommy standin' there holding that telegram." She sucked in a rattling sob. "Animals know. Got a secret eye that sees things humans can't. And now ... and now ... he knows that eye of his won't never see ..." She went over and began to stroke the dog. It looked at John Alan and growled.

"That's the pup Al gave Joe Bob, isn't it?" John Alan asked, sticking out his hand so the dog could smell it. "I'm a friend of Rachel's. She told me all about that pup. His name's Jeep, Jr., isn't it ... and you all call him J.J., don't you? Rachel's my really good friend."

"You know Al? Al's a good boy. A fine boy. He and Joe Bob done sports together ... baseball ... football ... basketball ... Joe Bob played it all."

"I ... I haven't lived here very long, but Rachel told me Joe Bob was the best quarterback ever! That's why ... that's why I brought you this present." He offered it to her again. "Please look at it," he begged. "It was made especially for you. It's going to protect Joe Bob."

"For me?" she repeated. "To protect Joe Bob?" Mrs. Snow stuck her hand out and took the box. She set it on the table and tried to open it without tearing the paper, but her burned fingers ripped it in places. She smoothed the jagged edges down and carefully folded the paper up, just as John Alan had done the day he received it. Then she opened the lid. "A gold angel with silver wings ..." she whispered as the tears started again. But this time they were quiet ones that made two little rivers down her wrinkled old cheeks. She slid down into a wooden chair at the stove end of the table.

John Alan had never felt so sad, not even when he found out that Toad had left them. "It's an angel, Mrs. Snow," he told her softly, "a football playing angel. The 'S' is for Snow." The lie slipped out real easy.

"I knowed that the minute I seen it," she said, tracing her fingernail around the "S" on the angel's chest. She laid the box gently on the table and pulled John Alan into her lap. He hadn't been held like that since his mother left, and it felt very nice. "I knowed that," she said over and over. "And that angel's gonna watch over my Joe Bob and bring him back to me."

She pointed to a cross with Jesus hanging from it which hung on the faded flowered wallpaper next to a yellow kitchen clock. "That man's already working on it, but even He can use help at a time like this."

She patted John Alan's head gently. "Jesus would have played quarterback, too, you know," she added with a knowing nod. "If they'd had football when He was a boy."

"Yes," John Alan said, grinning up at her, "I bet you're right."

***

She made him leave by the front door. He kept his eyes focused on the broken sidewalk and the grass growing up between the cracks. He didn't want to look in her victory garden or at that empty swing Joe Bob had promised to surprise them in.

CHAPTER 26
Home Again, Home Again

When he first heard the news about Joe Bob's death, John Alan thought about giving the angel to Rachel, but he couldn't think of a lie good enough to cover up where it had really come from. You sure didn't find something like that angel at the ten-cent store. He knew Rachel needed cheering up, but nothing he or Simon did worked for long. When Simon and his mother finally got a V-mail from his father, Rachel smiled for a few days, but that smile faded when they got word that her uncle Claude had been shipped out. She told them that her mother cried for three whole days.

"I asked my father about a million times how

they knew for sure Joe Bob is dead," she said as she stirred her Coke round and round with the straw, but didn't take a sip. They were the only three people in the drug store except for Mr. White and Elizabeth Cathcart. "He said Joe Bob's airplane took a direct hit . . . that there were witnesses. And that they were over the ocean when it happened. He says they sometimes make mistakes and say somebody's alive when they're really dead, but they don't say they're dead when they're alive."

John Alan wanted to tell her he knew for certain that what her father said was not true. That he personally knew of a woman who was reported to be dead when she was still very much alive. But he couldn't say that. Instead, he asked, "Where'd it happen? I heard my father say something about Midway Island. Midway to what?"

"Oh, I don't know. Way out the Pacific somewhere. You know how hard it is to get any real news. Everything's a military secret. It was a crazy coincidence my father found out as much as he did. A friend of his in Ardmore knew this guy whose family was at Pearl Harbor when it got bombed. The family is back there now, and they have friends in Hawaii who send them newspapers."

"It must take a million years to get mail from

Hawaii now," John Alan said, hoping to steer the conversation away from Joe Bob.

"This new V-mail's making it lots quicker, though," Simon chimed in. He knew what John Alan was trying to do. "My father writes a letter, and they take a picture that's littler than my thumbnail. That's what Mr. Kizer told my mother, anyway. It used to take thirty-seven mailbags to carry one hundred and fifty thousand one-page letters. Now they can put them all into one sack! Isn't that amazing?"

"You have to be the only kid in the world who could remember all that, Simon!" Rachel sighed. "But yeah, I guess it's pretty amazing. Too bad it's too late for Joe Bob," she added, biting her lip. "Paul and Al and I sat at this very booth with him the last time he was home, you know that?"

John Alan almost said, "Yeah, I remember every detail about that day," but since he'd been spying on Rachel and Paul, he didn't want to discuss it now. He needed to get her off the subject of Joe Bob entirely if he could, but he knew that once she got to talking about him, it was really hard to do.

"It took Joe Bob's letters about a hundred years to get to us." Tears were rimming her eyes again, "and we never were sure which ones of ours he got before ... before ..."

"Come on, Rachel," he pleaded, "drink your Coke so we can go. We've been in here long enough. Let's go take Jeep for a run!" He jumped out of the booth and gently tugged on her pigtail.

She picked up the glass and took a sip. "Free food at Carter's for The Duration! That's what Elizabeth told him Mr. White had said," she went on. There was no stopping her now. John Alan knew that. They had to let her finish this particular story, so he sat back down. "And Al told him ... Al told him if he could just drag the war out long enough ... if he could just keep on fighting the Germans forever ... he'd have free food for the rest of his— "

The bell on the front door of Carter's jangled, interrupting her. They were turning around to see who was coming in when they heard Mr. White bellow at the top of his lungs, "Holy Mary, Mother of God, it's Joe Bob! Joe Bob Snow! Mary Snow was right all along! They did make a mistake!"

CHAPTER 27
Christmas in July

Joe Bob made his miraculous appearance on a Monday, just in time to make the front page of Wednesday's *Republican*. Page one of many other state papers carried his picture, too, as the news of his survival of the Battle of Midway spread. Mr. Dalton, with the help of Rachel and John Alan, quickly revised the layout of the entire paper and bordered each page in stars. Stories about Joe Bob and pictures of him took up the entire front page. All that other news—Vera Marr's cat falling into the cistern, Mary McDaniel giving birth to twins—would have to wait until next week.

"Wish I could print those star borders in red,

white, and blue," Mr. Dalton told them over the clatter of the presses. "Be possible someday, I bet. Listen up, you two! Want to read you what I wrote." He stepped up on the wooden coal box by the door and bowed as if he were William Jennings Bryan about to deliver an oration. Rachel and John Alan applauded and cheered.

He began: "It was Christmas in July for local residents Mary and Sam Snow and their family when their oldest grandson, Private First Class Joe Bob Snow, became a modern day Lazarus and returned from the dead."

He lowered his copy and gave a self-satisfied sigh. "Pretty classy opening line, don't you think? Wouldn't be surprised if the UPI picked this one up!" John Alan knew Mr. Dalton's dream was to write an article worthy of UPI distribution, so he flashed him a V for victory sign. Mr. Dalton grinned and flashed a V himself before he returned to the article, which went like this:

Private Snow, who serves as a B-17E Tail Gunner, had been erroneously reported killed in action during the fierce attack on Midway Island early in the month; therefore, his entry into Carter's Drug Store at approximately 10:45 on

June 29 was an event equal to experiencing an earthquake.

"I had just gotten back from a slow roll to the bank and decided I'd stayed in the sun too long," Walter White, local pharmacist, laughed. Mr. White rides in a wheelchair due to a bout with polio, but he quickly realized that the sun had nothing to do with the amazing reunion he was witnessing in his drug store. Three local children, John Alan Feester, Jr., Simon Green, and Rachel Dalton, along with soda clerk Elizabeth Cathcart, made sure they were not seeing a ghost by giving the young soldier all the punches, slaps on the back, and hugs he could stand. Elizabeth and Rachel even resorted to kissing him "just to be sure he was alive" they explained.

"John Steinbeck could put that reunion scene in his next novel," Young Mr. Green reported. "It was as good as anything in *The Moon Is Down*." Young Mr. Green knows his novels, as he is the son of well-known mystery writer Isadore Green, who is now serving in the United States Navy. The other two youngsters agreed. Naturally, the crowd was thirsty for details of Private Snow's survival, but they were even more eager to see the faces of the Snow grand-parents, who have been grieving their loss.

Mr. White wisely decided that the children should fetch Dr. Inman to accompany Joe Bob on his triumphant re-entry into his grandparents' lives since the Snows are elderly and the shock might cause them to need medical attention. He also cautioned everyone to allow Joe Bob to greet his family privately before the rest of the town became involved.

The happy reunion was accomplished in short order without the doctor having to administer smelling salts to any of those involved.

"I never believed he was dead!" Mrs. Snow stated emphatically. "That boy had lots of help from up there," she added pointing her finger toward heaven, which indeed, must have been intimately involved. She reported that she had been looking out her kitchen window when she spied Joe Bob attempting to sneak into her garden and slip into the swing located there. It seems that when he left on New Year's Day, he promised he would return to that garden and that swing unnoticed and wait to be discovered.

While military blackout rules concerning war forbade Private Snow from giving details, he was able to relate the following: after surviving the downing of his plane, he spent several days in a raft before being rescued. He was then taken by ship to Hawaii and flown back to the United States. He was granted a two-week furlough at that time. Unaware that his family had been notified of his death, he decided that rather than waste money on an expensive long distance telephone call or telegram, he would surprise them with a visit. Surprise them he did.

Mr. Dalton put the paper down and waited for John Alan and Rachel's reaction.

"That was wonderful, Daddy. If the UPI doesn't grab up that one, they're crazy!" Rachel went over and hugged his neck, and John Alan wished he could do that, too, but none of the boys he knew did things like that. Not to somebody else's father anyway. He picked up one of the papers as it slipped off the press and smelled the damp ink before he began to read.

There was a separate story about the dirt. The headline on that column read "A Prince of a Fellow." John Alan was glad Rachel finally got to hear about that dirt from Mrs. Snow's garden. *He* certainly hadn't been able to tell her since he'd gotten the information by eavesdropping on her very own brother.

Since Al hadn't told her, John Alan sure didn't want to be the one to let the cat out of the bag—or Prince Albert out of the can either.

He began to read. Joe Bob told of having the can in his pocket when he bailed out of his plane. He said that during the long, lonely hours he had waited to be picked up, that can of dirt was the one thing left in the world that kept him going—smelling and feeling that dirt from his grandmother's garden, sprinkling it between his toes, and dreaming about walking on it again. It was a fine story. A really fine story.

The final front-page story concerned the upcoming wedding of Joe Bob Snow and Miss Mae Ella Cathcart. It was to take place at 2:00 on Sunday, July 5, in the American Legion Hall. That was the only place big enough to hold the expected crowd, since the whole town was invited. They weren't even going to bother with chairs, so everyone was warned to expect to stand for the ceremony. A reception and pounding were to be held in the basement after the promises were exchanged.

"We're planning a super, colossal, stupendous Fourth of July celebration for next Saturday," John Alan heard Mr. Dalton telling Rachel. They were back in the little closet room where they kept the old files. "Pull the paper for July 2 last year, would you?

Want to see what I wrote about the parade when war was still just brewing. All I remember is that Sam Sing was going to carry the flag, as always. Glad the Fourth's on Saturday this year so the farmers can come. Too busy in the fields to take a weekday off, but now some of them can decorate their tractors and join us. Gasoline is scarce, but since Joe Bob's going to be leading the parade, we need to have one hundred percent participation this year."

"Then I'm going to see to it that Mr. B. Arnold Johnson flies a flag!" Rachel declared, grabbing a copy of the paper off the press as she stomped toward the door. "You guys follow me!"

CHAPTER 28
B. Arnold Johnson's Secret

"You got a grandma and grandpa, Mr. Johnson?" they heard Rachel inquire in a sugary sweet voice after she'd paid for her pop and followed the station owner inside. They had to crouch under the front window of the Flying Red Horse to listen since Rachel had informed them in no uncertain terms that getting Mr. B. Arnold Johnson to fly a flag on the Fourth of July was "women's work."

"A grandma and grandpa?" he replied, sounding extremely suspicious. "What kinda question is that?

'Course I had a grandma and grandpa. Everbody's got relatives like that." There was a pause where they couldn't tell what was going on before he growled, "Now you get on with you. I got work to do."

"What'd you call 'em?" Rachel pressed, and they heard her slurping a loud slow slurp from her Grapette soda to make it last longer.

"Well ... well ... ya see I couldn't talk very good to begin with so the names I called 'em were stupid." They heard a drawer get jerked open and then get slammed shut.

"I won't think they're stupid," Rachel assured him in the same syrupy tone. "Tell me, and I promise I won't even giggle." The boys shoved their hands in their mouths so they wouldn't laugh and ruin her whole plan. They had crossed their hearts and hoped to die that they'd keep quiet if she'd just let them eavesdrop.

"Mebo," Mr. Johnson stammered. "Mebo and Pepo. That's what I called 'em ... don't remember why ..." His voice trailed away as if he hadn't thought of those names in a very long time. "They were good people ... good, kind people." John Alan mouthed "Mebo" and "Pepo" and then rolled his eyes, but when Mr. Johnson added the "good people" remark, the smile on his face faded. B. Arnold Johnson wasn't all bad either.

"Well, I think Mebo and Pepo are great names! One-of-a kind names! Bet they were a one-of-a-kind grandma and grandpa, too."

"Why you all a sudden interested in my family, Red?" B. Arnold Johnson asked. The boys' eyes popped wide open. Now he'd done it!

"Oh, I don't know ... I just been thinking a lot about grandmas and grandpas cause of Mr. and Mrs. Snow, and all they been through lately. My mama says they're too old to have to be raising a bunch of kids."

"Good people do what they gotta do, and the Snows are good people. I watch 'em out the window of my station. Old man like that ... playing ball with those boys. Old lady, too. I've watched her trying to catch those boys' passes and such ... all of 'em laughing and smiling." There was a long pause before he asked, "You seen him yet? That Snow boy?"

"Sure, I was right there in Carter's when he walked in! I was the first one to hug him! Here ... here's a copy of my Daddy's paper, hot off the press! I thought you might like to read about how it happened. Knew you didn't subscribe to the paper, so this one's a present from me to you!"

There was another pause, the longest one yet. "Would ... would you mind reading it to me, Red?

You see ... you see ... that's one thing I never learned to do," B. Arnold Johnson admitted in a soft, sad voice. "And I sure would like to know all about what happened to that boy. I sure would."

Rachel cleared her throat and began to read as John Alan and Simon, shaking their heads, sneaked away.

Mr. Johnson would be flying his flag. They didn't need to stick around to know that, and they sure needed to talk.

CHAPTER 29
America the Beautiful

"But next to the one you had last year, of course, don't you think *this* Fourth of July was probably the best one since 1776, Simon?" Rachel asked, heaving a big sigh. John Alan knew she wasn't looking for an answer. Most of Rachel's questions were like that. She asked them when she was getting ready to tell a story herself, but he didn't mind that. Not anymore.

Actually, he was glad she was about to launch into something. Simon had just finished telling them in detail about his Fourth of July last year back in Pennsylvania, a really great day because his father was still home and his whole family, even his dog, had gone camping. When Simon finished, John Alan was afraid they might expect him to be the next story-teller, so he was relieved when Rachel jumped in with her 1776 remark.

He and Simon and Al were sitting on the back porch of Rachel's grandparents' house in Cyril, where they had driven after the big parade. It had been real crowded with four kids in the back seat, but it had been a lot of fun, too, because they sang songs for the whole ten miles.

He was glad his father had gone to California to "check on some business," because Simon's mother had talked Mr. Feester into letting John Alan stay with them while he was gone. Then, when the Daltons invited them all for a Fourth of July picnic supper, he felt like he was part of a real family. At least for a little while.

"Speaking of 1776 and wars ..." Rachel began.

He knew it. She had some Revolutionary War story she was going to tell, but she'd change every-thing around to suit her own fancy, like saying people were spies when they really weren't.

"Speaking of 1776 and wars," she repeated, "Al, my good and wise big brother, I want you to explain to me why *men* are always wanting to go fight wars?

Why is that, anyway? I find everything about war very enigmaing."

John Alan was quite sure he was the only one who knew what she meant. After all, he was her very own "big fat enigma," wasn't he? He didn't want to break their truce, but he did feel the need to set her straight.

"Well, Miss Dictionary Mouth, far be it from me to correct an expert like you, but there's no such word as enigmaing. Enigma means a puzzle, but you can't stick 'ing' on it. Enigmatic is the word you're looking for." He tried not to smirk. "Enigmatic means very puzzling. That's the word you're searching for."

"Well, excuse me! I stand corrected by the world's most belligerent—"

"Hey, now, you two," Simon broke in, pulling a white handkerchief from his pocket and waving it at them. "You've been so good lately ... You declared a truce for The Duration. The Duration has not come yet."

"They ought to stick you on the next boat to Europe, Simon," Al told him. "Anybody smart enough to get these two together ought to be working for Uncle Sam. But to answer your question, Red, I find it enigmatic myself that I want to go to war, but I do. I want to real bad."

Everybody got quiet for a while, but finally Al broke the silence. "Remember all the fun you and Paul always had at these picnics? Like that time you decided to act out that picture of the fife and drum guys . . . that one in everybody's history books?" He turned to Simon and John Alan. John Alan looked at Rachel and groaned. They both knew what was coming.

"Yes, indeed," Simon replied, giving his usual knowing nod. "Actually, that picture has two titles— 'Yankee Doodle' and 'Spirit of '76.' The artist was Archibald Willard, whose father was the model for the older gentleman in the middle of the three. His name was Samuel Willard, and he was a minister. The original was an eight-by-ten-inch oil done in 1875—"

"I knew that!" Al interrupted, almost doubling over laughing. He'd heard all about Simon, but this was the first time he'd seen him in action. "I knew all of that, but I didn't want to bore you with a lot of dry facts."

Simon shrugged and went back to petting Shorty, the old hound dog whose tail was thumping on the boards of the hot, dry porch.

"I'd forgotten that!" Rachel said, sounding as if she were about to cry. "Paul played the little drummer boy, and we couldn't find a piece of white material for the bandage, so Gram just tied two of Gunny's white socks together and wrapped them around Paul's head. The toe hung right over one eye, and he kept trying to blow it away so he could see where he was going .. I wonder if he remembers that?"

"Rachel played a wooden spoon fife and made the rest of us fall in behind her. She ordered poor old Gunny to carry the flag, and we all had to march around the house four times because it was the Fourth of July," Al told Simon and John Alan.

"We stood at attention and saluted while Gunny hung the flag from the front porch eave, and then we all sang 'The Star Spangled Banner' before we ate ice cream and cake till it was too dark to find our mouths with our spoons." Al got up and went over and stood in front of Rachel. He caught her chin in his hand and looked her right in the eyes.

"I guess that's why I want to go to war, Rachel. Why all men do. So the people they love can march on the Fourth of July. So they can hang their American flags from the front porch anytime they want to. So everybody can sing 'The Star Spangled Banner' whether they're good singers or not. I even want to go to war so we can have cake and ice cream again."

He sat back down. The sky was turning that shade of bruised purple it gets just before the sun drops below the horizon, so they all just sat and waited for the dark to finish riding over the edge of the world.

"Hey, you guys! Soup's on! Come fill your plates!" Rachel's father called from the kitchen, breaking the silence and scattering their Fourth of July memories all over the summer-dried grass.

CHAPTER 30
The Long Way Home

John Alan knew something was wrong when his father called and told Mrs. Green to send him home and didn't even ask to speak to him. John Alan and Simon were in the living room when the phone rang, so he could hear Mrs. Green's end of the conversation. The call was very short—so short, in fact, that John Alan wondered if his father even thanked her for letting him stay at their house for a whole week.

Instead of going straight home, he rode his bicycle in bigger and bigger squares around the blocks between his and Simon's houses. He did the block that surrounded the school twice, honking his horn at Mr.

Johnson, who was pumping gas and washing the windows of Miss Oxley's old Ford, both times. He pointed at Mr. Johnson's flag and gave him the old thumbs up. He even waved at Odious Oxley, who was now teaching Mr. Johnson to read. That had been Rachel's doing. Rachel now called Mr. B. Arnold Johnson "Arnie."

Finally, John Alan decided his father was going to be really mad at him for taking so long, so he headed home. He put his bike in the garage, being careful not to scratch the side of their shiny blue Buick, and went inside. He could hear his father slamming the refrigerator door hard, so he headed for the kitchen and whatever troubles were sitting at their table that day.

"Sit down, John Alan," his father commanded as John Alan walked through the door. "I have to talk to you. I have some news about your mother."

His father didn't come over and hug him, he didn't say he missed him, he didn't smile and ruffle his hair. But then, he never did things like that. Never.

John Alan sat down in one of the brightly painted red kitchen chairs. The other two were black, but the red ones were his and his mother's. He gripped the sides of the seat with both hands.

His father did not sit down. He walked very slowly to the head of the table and stood behind the black chair he always sat in—even after they had moved here. Why do people always sit at the same places at a table? John Alan found himself wondering. That day when Mrs. Snow held him in her lap, she said she hadn't moved Joe Bob's chair since he left, not even to mop under it. John Alan decided if he could just keep thinking about chairs, he wouldn't have to think about what his father was about to tell him.

"She ... she ... she wants to come back to us," Mr. John Alan Feester, Sr., stammered. "And ... and ... I said it would be all right."

John Alan felt as if that silver and gold angel had just launched the longest pass ever attempted in the entire history of Stanford football ... no, wait ... make that the longest pass ever attempted in the entire world ... and that he, John Alan Feester, Jr., had just caught it! He jumped out of the red chair, knocking it over backwards. Then he ran over to his father, threw his arms around his waist, and buried his face in his chest.

John Alan Feester, Sr., hugged him back, ruffled his hair, and began to sob.

She was coming back!

And there was nobody he could tell.

* * *

"There are still a lot of details to be worked out," his father told him as they ate their supper that night. "It ... it ... wasn't another man ... it ... it was me." He stirred his macaroni and cheese around on his plate. "She ... she was raised on a farm in Nebraska and came into this marriage with a different set of standards, a different set of ... expectations." He looked up at John Alan. "But none of that concerns you," he added abruptly. "What does concern you is our position in this town. You do realize that you can never, ever tell any of these people she's alive, don't you?"

"But Dad! What about my friends? They'd understand! They can keep secrets, I know they can! Look how happy everybody was to find out that Joe Bob Snow was alive when they thought he was dead!"

His father got up, walked around the table and got the other red chair—his mother's chair—and pulled it up to face John Alan. He sat down and grabbed him by both shoulders.

"Now listen to me, son, and listen well. Our situation is nothing at all like Joe Bob Snow's. I'm going to be resigning from my job here just before school is ready to start again. Due to the shortage of qualified men these days, that's going to leave this town in a real bind. What kind of recommendation do you think I'd get from this school board if they found out I lied on my application?"

"But—"

"There is no room for argument, here, John Alan. I took a job in the defense plant where your mother is working while I was out there last week, but when the war is over I'll want to get back into education. My chances would be severely damaged if these people found out the truth now. I'll tell them I'm doing it for the money. And for you to be closer to your grandparents. They'll accept that. I never should have lied to begin with. But ... but ... at the time I was so ... I thought ..." He got up and left the room.

John Alan started to follow him, but he decided against it. He knew his father was right, but he sure wished he could at least tell Rachel and Simon why he was moving away so quickly. "Three may keep a secret if two of them are dead," he said to the empty red chair across from him. "Guess you and me and Dad are going to have to prove old Ben Franklin was wrong, aren't we, Mother?" He walked around to her chair and patted the back gently with both hands. Then he sat down in it and began to cry.

CHAPTER 31
Final "Aid and Comfort"

"Well, Rachel, guess you're going to go testify against those German saboteurs tomorrow, aren't you?" John Alan joked as they all three stood in front of the moving van. "Give 'em a little 'aid and comfort' maybe? All eight of those guys go on trial tomorrow, you know. Hope the car radio'll pick up the news. Fades in and out an awful lot on a long trip like this one." He picked up a dry twig and began to break it in little pieces.

"They won't get any 'aid and comfort' from anybody around here," Rachel told him, her eyes getting as big as Annie's, as usual. He was going to miss those big eyes of hers. The rest of her face, too, for that matter. "Not after what they were planning to do to the United States of America! My daddy says if they find them guilty, they'll electrocute them before the week's out!"

"Can they do that?" Simon wanted to know. "That quickly, I mean."

"Daddy says they can and they will, and he knows all about that kind of stuff just like J.A. here knows about football," she punched him on the arm and bit her lip. "Oh, I sure do hope I didn't injure your passing arm! We're gonna hear about you playing quarterback for one of those fancy California schools someday, aren't we? You ought to come back here if you're gonna play football. The game was invented in Oklahoma, you know!"

"Sure, Rachel, sure, we all know how good you are at getting your facts straight. Football was invented in Oklahoma, I had something to do with Pearl Harbor, and Mr. Johnson's great-grandfather was Benedict Arnold. If you want to get your facts straight, just give old Rachel Elizabeth Dalton, otherwise known as Red, a call. She knows it all!"

"We're about ready to go, John Alan," his father called as he slammed the trunk of their Buick. The three friends took turns looking at each other and sighing.

"You gonna write to us?" Rachel asked, drawing dust circles with her big toe and chewing on one pigtail. She was blinking real hard.

John Alan just nodded. His father had said he'd be allowed to write, at least for a while. If he was careful what he talked about. But he knew as time went by, the letters would stop. They always do. California was a long way from Oklahoma, and, because of his mother, he was certain they'd never come back for a visit. That was going to be the hardest part—not ever knowing what happened to any of these people. Joe Bob Snow, Simon's father, even Odious Oxley—he was losing them all forever. But compared to losing his mother ...

"You know the only reason I'm allowing you to move is because I made a deal with the governor of California, don't you? He and my father are close personal friends. That's why I was able to trade you for Paul," Rachel prattled. "That's ... that's the way it works during war. Kind of a prisoner exchange, it was." She began to pick up the little pieces of the stick he had been dropping and put them in her pocket.

"I'm real glad he's moving back, Rachel," John Alan told her, handing her what was left of the stick. "That way everybody ends up happy, don't they?"

217

"Sure, J.A.," Simon growled. "This whole war's just been filled with one happy moment after another so far." He began to stomp on some red ants that were making their way toward Rachel's bare toes. "You're about to get stung big time, Rachel. Told you to put on your shoes!' He looked at John Alan and tried to smile, but the smile slid right off the edge of his mouth before he could finish it. "Now about the truce," he went on, "since you're having to leave before The Duration, I believe that the two of you should—"

"That's it, son! Time to go! That forty-mile-an-hour speed limit is going to make this trip seem like forever! You kids take care of yourselves, now!" He flashed them a V for victory sign as he climbed into the car.

John Alan hit Simon on the shoulder real hard, harder than he'd ever hit him before, but Simon didn't hit him back. He didn't even look up. He just kept stomping those ants.

"Well, good-bye, Simon. Help Rachel keep her nose clean, okay? I remember the first time I saw her, she was picking it!"

"Why you . . . you Big Fat Enigma you! You were the one who—"

John Alan interrupted her by doing something

he'd never done to a girl in his life, except his mother, of course. He grabbed Rachel by the shoulders and kissed her. Right on the mouth.

"I ... I ... gotta go ... right *now* ... and that ... that was the only way I could think of to shut you up," he stammered, stepping back quickly. "Besides, you looked like you could use ... a little aid and comfort. Don't you agree, Simon?"

Simon was too busy stomping ants to look up or answer.

Epilogue

The third and final Friday the thirteenth in 1942, the one in November, turned out to be a lucky day for Simon Green's father and the United States Navy. Although Mr. Green was injured badly enough that he was sent back to the United States to recuperate, he did survive the naval Battle of Guadalcanal, which was waged November 12–15. His battleship, the USS *Washington*, was one of two American ships involved. The other was the USS *South Dakota*. The radar-directed fire from the 16-inch guns of those ships helped to destroy two Japanese battleships, a cruiser, two destroyers, and ten transports. The victory ensured the success of American ground forces on Guadalcanal. On February 7, 1943, the last of the Japanese left the island.

It was many months before Simon learned that his father had been injured on Friday the thirteenth, but the fact that Isadore Green survived proved that, once again, Simon was right. As he told Jean Margaret way back in January, triskaidekaphobia is "nothing but a silly superstition with no truth in it."

And truth, as John Alan Feester, Jr., came to know, is a vital ingredient in any story.

Author's Note
Real People in the Real War

The story of Joe Bob Snow's amazing return from the "dead" is loosely based on a true story related to me by Jean Sims of Apache, my own hometown. Her family, like hundreds of thousands across the world, was permanently scarred by WWII but with a bit of a different twist. In 1939 her musically gifted, pet-of-the-family young brother joined the Marine Corps at her father's suggestion so he would be able to continue his education when he was released. That release was to come in February of 1942.

Ovid Walter Campbell, the sixth of seven children and the youngest boy, attended boot camp in San Diego and played French horn in the Marine Marching Band, which made the family very proud as he had never played a brass instrument until he became a Marine. Although he was in the United States for quite some time, he never had a leave long enough to enable him to come home. Mrs. Sims wrote: "The family all missed him a lot. Although most of them had left home, all his siblings were in Oklahoma. And Ovid was so very far away."

After serving a tour of duty in Colorado, he was sent to the Philippines in early 1941. By fall, he had made lance corporal and was acting sergeant. Then, on December 7, the world was blown apart, and Ovid's family never heard from him again.

It was not until August of 1942 that the Campbells received a "missing in action" telegram, and not until May of 1943 that the final "killed in action" notice arrived. The frantic family had done everything they knew to do during the intervening time—contacted congressmen, written government agencies, and so on—so the final word allowed them to face the horrible truth at last.

"Mother traded one of the blue stars in the window for gold," Mrs. Sims wrote, "and buried her grief deep inside her to try to help my father."

The wait for the truth had been a long one, but the real pain for the Campbell family was just beginning. Within weeks of their final notice, their neighbors in the tiny Oklahoma town of Welch also got a "killed in action" telegram concerning their son, who coincidentally had also been in the Philippines.

Three weeks later, the neighbors' son walked in the door of his parents' house. The telegrams about him had been wrong.

"That created a hope in my family which proved to be futile. My father retreated to his bedroom and sat for hours doing nothing and rarely moving. He preached twice on Sundays (Eugene Campbell was a Baptist minister) but did very little pastoral work after that time," Mrs. Sims remembered.

The family never gave up their hope that what had happened to the boy next door had also happened to their son, that he would walk in their front door and surprise them at any moment.

"There is no such thing as closure," Mrs. Sims wrote.

It is hoped, however, that having Ovid Walter Campbell's name and story in a book that teachers will be reading to their classes, that grandparents will be reading to their grandchildren, and that children themselves will be reading will bring a warm memory to the hearts of those he left behind such a long time ago.

Perpetual Calendar

A **perpetual calendar** lets you find the day of the week for any date in any year. Since January 1 may fall on any of the seven days of the week, and may be a leap or non-leap year, 14 different calendars are possible. The number next to each year corresponds to one of the 14 calendars.

Year	No.	Year	No.	Year	No.	Year	No.	Year	No.	Year	No.	Year	No.
1775	1	1815	1	1855	2	1895	3	1935	3	1975	4	2015	5
1776	9	1816	9	1856	10	1896	11	1936	11	1976	12	2016	13
1777	4	1817	4	1857	5	1897	6	1937	6	1977	7	2017	1
1778	5	1818	5	1858	6	1898	7	1938	7	1978	1	2018	2
1779	6	1819	6	1859	7	1899	1	1939	1	1979	2	2019	3
1780	14	1820	14	1860	8	1900	2	1940	9	1980	10	2020	11
1781	2	1821	2	1861	3	1901	3	1941	4	1981	5	2021	6
1782	3	1822	3	1862	4	1902	4	1942	5	1982	6	2022	7
1783	4	1823	4	1863	5	1903	5	1943	6	1983	7	2023	1
1784	12	1824	12	1864	13	1904	13	1944	14	1984	8	2024	9
1785	7	1825	7	1865	1	1905	1	1945	2	1985	3	2025	4
1786	1	1826	1	1866	2	1906	2	1946	3	1986	4	2026	5
1787	2	1827	2	1867	3	1907	3	1947	4	1987	5	2027	6
1788	10	1828	10	1868	11	1908	11	1948	12	1988	13	2028	14
1789	5	1829	5	1869	6	1909	6	1949	7	1989	1	2029	2
1790	6	1830	6	1870	7	1910	7	1950	1	1990	2	2030	3
1791	7	1831	7	1871	1	1911	1	1951	2	1991	3	2031	4
1792	8	1832	8	1872	9	1912	9	1952	10	1992	11	2032	12
1793	3	1833	3	1873	4	1913	4	1953	5	1993	6	2033	7
1794	4	1834	4	1874	5	1914	5	1954	6	1994	7	2034	1
1795	5	1835	5	1875	6	1915	6	1955	7	1995	1	2035	2
1796	13	1836	13	1876	14	1916	14	1956	8	1996	9	2036	10
1797	1	1837	1	1877	2	1917	2	1957	3	1997	4	2037	5
1798	2	1838	2	1878	3	1918	3	1958	4	1998	5	2038	6
1799	3	1839	3	1879	4	1919	4	1959	5	1999	6	2039	7
1800	4	1840	11	1880	12	1920	12	1960	13	2000	14	2040	8
1801	5	1841	6	1881	7	1921	7	1961	1	2001	2	2041	3
1802	6	1842	7	1882	1	1922	1	1962	2	2002	3	2042	4
1803	7	1843	1	1883	2	1923	2	1963	3	2003	4	2043	5
1804	8	1844	9	1884	10	1924	10	1964	11	2004	12	2044	13
1805	3	1845	4	1885	5	1925	5	1965	6	2005	7	2045	1
1806	4	1846	5	1886	6	1926	6	1966	7	2006	1	2046	2
1807	5	1847	6	1887	7	1927	7	1967	1	2007	2	2047	3
1808	13	1848	14	1888	8	1928	8	1968	9	2008	10	2048	11
1809	1	1849	2	1889	3	1929	3	1969	4	2009	5	2049	6
1810	2	1850	3	1890	4	1930	4	1970	5	2010	6	2050	7
1811	3	1851	4	1891	5	1931	5	1971	6	2011	7		
1812	11	1852	12	1892	13	1932	13	1972	14	2012	8		
1813	6	1853	7	1893	1	1933	1	1973	2	2013	3		
1814	7	1854	1	1894	2	1934	2	1974	3	2014	4		

1

JANUARY
```
S  M  T  W  T  F  S
       1  2  3  4  5
 6  7  8  9 10 11 12
13 14 15 16 17 18 19
20 21 22 23 24 25 26
27 28 29 30 31
```
FEBRUARY
```
S  M  T  W  T  F  S
                1  2
 3  4  5  6  7  8  9
10 11 12 13 14 15 16
17 18 19 20 21 22 23
24 25 26 27 28
```
MARCH
```
S  M  T  W  T  F  S
                1  2
 3  4  5  6  7  8  9
10 11 12 13 14 15 16
17 18 19 20 21 22 23
24 25 26 27 28 29 30
31
```
APRIL
```
S  M  T  W  T  F  S
    1  2  3  4  5  6
 7  8  9 10 11 12 13
14 15 16 17 18 19 20
21 22 23 24 25 26 27
28 29 30
```
MAY
```
S  M  T  W  T  F  S
          1  2  3  4
 5  6  7  8  9 10 11
12 13 14 15 16 17 18
19 20 21 22 23 24 25
26 27 28 29 30 31
```
JUNE
```
S  M  T  W  T  F  S
                   1
 2  3  4  5  6  7  8
 9 10 11 12 13 14 15
16 17 18 19 20 21 22
23 24 25 26 27 28 29
30
```
JULY
```
S  M  T  W  T  F  S
    1  2  3  4  5  6
 7  8  9 10 11 12 13
14 15 16 17 18 19 20
21 22 23 24 25 26 27
28 29 30 31
```
AUGUST
```
S  M  T  W  T  F  S
             1  2  3
 4  5  6  7  8  9 10
11 12 13 14 15 16 17
18 19 20 21 22 23 24
25 26 27 28 29 30 31
```
SEPTEMBER
```
S  M  T  W  T  F  S
 1  2  3  4  5  6  7
 8  9 10 11 12 13 14
15 16 17 18 19 20 21
22 23 24 25 26 27 28
29 30
```
OCTOBER
```
S  M  T  W  T  F  S
       1  2  3  4  5
 6  7  8  9 10 11 12
13 14 15 16 17 18 19
20 21 22 23 24 25 26
27 28 29 30 31
```
NOVEMBER
```
S  M  T  W  T  F  S
                1  2
 3  4  5  6  7  8  9
10 11 12 13 14 15 16
17 18 19 20 21 22 23
24 25 26 27 28 29 30
```
DECEMBER
```
S  M  T  W  T  F  S
 1  2  3  4  5  6  7
 8  9 10 11 12 13 14
15 16 17 18 19 20 21
22 23 24 25 26 27 28
29 30 31
```

2

JANUARY
```
S  M  T  W  T  F  S
    1  2  3  4  5  6
 7  8  9 10 11 12 13
14 15 16 17 18 19 20
21 22 23 24 25 26 27
28 29 30 31
```
FEBRUARY
```
S  M  T  W  T  F  S
             1  2  3
 4  5  6  7  8  9 10
11 12 13 14 15 16 17
18 19 20 21 22 23 24
25 26 27 28
```
MARCH
```
S  M  T  W  T  F  S
             1  2  3
 4  5  6  7  8  9 10
11 12 13 14 15 16 17
18 19 20 21 22 23 24
25 26 27 28 29 30 31
```
APRIL
```
S  M  T  W  T  F  S
 1  2  3  4  5  6  7
 8  9 10 11 12 13 14
15 16 17 18 19 20 21
22 23 24 25 26 27 28
29 30
```
MAY
```
S  M  T  W  T  F  S
          1  2  3  4
 5  6  7  8  9 10 11
12 13 14 15 16 17 18
19 20 21 22 23 24 25
26 27 28 29 30 31
```
JUNE
```
S  M  T  W  T  F  S
                1  2
 3  4  5  6  7  8  9
10 11 12 13 14 15 16
17 18 19 20 21 22 23
24 25 26 27 28 29 30
```
JULY
```
S  M  T  W  T  F  S
 1  2  3  4  5  6  7
 8  9 10 11 12 13 14
15 16 17 18 19 20 21
22 23 24 25 26 27 28
29 30 31
```
AUGUST
```
S  M  T  W  T  F  S
       1  2  3  4
 5  6  7  8  9 10 11
12 13 14 15 16 17 18
19 20 21 22 23 24 25
26 27 28 29 30 31
```
SEPTEMBER
```
S  M  T  W  T  F  S
                   1
 2  3  4  5  6  7  8
 9 10 11 12 13 14 15
16 17 18 19 20 21 22
23 24 25 26 27 28 29
30
```
OCTOBER
```
S  M  T  W  T  F  S
    1  2  3  4  5  6
 7  8  9 10 11 12 13
14 15 16 17 18 19 20
21 22 23 24 25 26 27
28 29 30 31
```
NOVEMBER
```
S  M  T  W  T  F  S
             1  2  3
 4  5  6  7  8  9 10
11 12 13 14 15 16 17
18 19 20 21 22 23 24
25 26 27 28 29 30
```
DECEMBER
```
S  M  T  W  T  F  S
                   1
 2  3  4  5  6  7  8
 9 10 11 12 13 14 15
16 17 18 19 20 21 22
23 24 25 26 27 28 29
30 31
```

3

JANUARY
```
 S  M  T  W  T  F  S
          1  2  3  4  5
 6  7  8  9 10 11 12
13 14 15 16 17 18 19
20 21 22 23 24 25 26
27 28 29 30 31
```
FEBRUARY
```
 S  M  T  W  T  F  S
                1  2
 3  4  5  6  7  8  9
10 11 12 13 14 15 16
17 18 19 20 21 22 23
24 25 26 27 28
```
MARCH
```
 S  M  T  W  T  F  S
                1  2
 3  4  5  6  7  8  9
10 11 12 13 14 15 16
17 18 19 20 21 22 23
24 25 26 27 28 29 30
31
```
APRIL
```
 S  M  T  W  T  F  S
    1  2  3  4  5  6
 7  8  9 10 11 12 13
14 15 16 17 18 19 20
21 22 23 24 25 26 27
28 29 30
```
MAY
```
 S  M  T  W  T  F  S
          1  2  3  4
 5  6  7  8  9 10 11
12 13 14 15 16 17 18
19 20 21 22 23 24 25
26 27 28 29 30 31
```
JUNE
```
 S  M  T  W  T  F  S
                   1
 2  3  4  5  6  7  8
 9 10 11 12 13 14 15
16 17 18 19 20 21 22
23 24 25 26 27 28 29
30
```
JULY
```
 S  M  T  W  T  F  S
    1  2  3  4  5  6
 7  8  9 10 11 12 13
14 15 16 17 18 19 20
21 22 23 24 25 26 27
28 29 30 31
```
AUGUST
```
 S  M  T  W  T  F  S
             1  2  3
 4  5  6  7  8  9 10
11 12 13 14 15 16 17
18 19 20 21 22 23 24
25 26 27 28 29 30 31
```
SEPTEMBER
```
 S  M  T  W  T  F  S
 1  2  3  4  5  6  7
 8  9 10 11 12 13 14
15 16 17 18 19 20 21
22 23 24 25 26 27 28
29 30
```
OCTOBER
```
 S  M  T  W  T  F  S
          1  2  3  4  5
 6  7  8  9 10 11 12
13 14 15 16 17 18 19
20 21 22 23 24 25 26
27 28 29 30 31
```
NOVEMBER
```
 S  M  T  W  T  F  S
                1  2
 3  4  5  6  7  8  9
10 11 12 13 14 15 16
17 18 19 20 21 22 23
24 25 26 27 28 29 30
```
DECEMBER
```
 S  M  T  W  T  F  S
 1  2  3  4  5  6  7
 8  9 10 11 12 13 14
15 16 17 18 19 20 21
22 23 24 25 26 27 28
29 30 31
```

4

JANUARY
```
 S  M  T  W  T  F  S
             1  2  3  4
 5  6  7  8  9 10 11
12 13 14 15 16 17 18
19 20 21 22 23 24 25
26 27 28 29 30 31
```
FEBRUARY
```
 S  M  T  W  T  F  S
                   1
 2  3  4  5  6  7  8
 9 10 11 12 13 14 15
16 17 18 19 20 21 22
23 24 25 26 27 28
```
MARCH
```
 S  M  T  W  T  F  S
                   1
 2  3  4  5  6  7  8
 9 10 11 12 13 14 15
16 17 18 19 20 21 22
23 24 25 26 27 28 29
30 31
```
APRIL
```
 S  M  T  W  T  F  S
          1  2  3  4  5
 6  7  8  9 10 11 12
13 14 15 16 17 18 19
20 21 22 23 24 25 26
27 28 29 30
```
MAY
```
 S  M  T  W  T  F  S
             1  2  3
 4  5  6  7  8  9 10
11 12 13 14 15 16 17
18 19 20 21 22 23 24
25 26 27 28 29 30 31
```
JUNE
```
 S  M  T  W  T  F  S
 1  2  3  4  5  6  7
 8  9 10 11 12 13 14
15 16 17 18 19 20 21
22 23 24 25 26 27 28
29 30
```
JULY
```
 S  M  T  W  T  F  S
          1  2  3  4  5
 6  7  8  9 10 11 12
13 14 15 16 17 18 19
20 21 22 23 24 25 26
27 28 29 30 31
```
AUGUST
```
 S  M  T  W  T  F  S
                1  2
 3  4  5  6  7  8  9
10 11 12 13 14 15 16
17 18 19 20 21 22 23
24 25 26 27 28 29 30
31
```
SEPTEMBER
```
 S  M  T  W  T  F  S
    1  2  3  4  5  6
 7  8  9 10 11 12 13
14 15 16 17 18 19 20
21 22 23 24 25 26 27
28 29 30
```
OCTOBER
```
 S  M  T  W  T  F  S
             1  2  3  4
 5  6  7  8  9 10 11
12 13 14 15 16 17 18
19 20 21 22 23 24 25
26 27 28 29 30 31
```
NOVEMBER
```
 S  M  T  W  T  F  S
                   1
 2  3  4  5  6  7  8
 9 10 11 12 13 14 15
16 17 18 19 20 21 22
23 24 25 26 27 28 29
30
```
DECEMBER
```
 S  M  T  W  T  F  S
    1  2  3  4  5  6
 7  8  9 10 11 12 13
14 15 16 17 18 19 20
21 22 23 24 25 26 27
28 29 30 31
```

5

JANUARY
```
 S  M  T  W  T  F  S
             1  2  3
 4  5  6  7  8  9 10
11 12 13 14 15 16 17
18 19 20 21 22 23 24
25 26 27 28 29 30 31
```
FEBRUARY
```
 S  M  T  W  T  F  S
 1  2  3  4  5  6  7
 8  9 10 11 12 13 14
15 16 17 18 19 20 21
22 23 24 25 26 27 28
```
MARCH
```
 S  M  T  W  T  F  S
 1  2  3  4  5  6  7
 8  9 10 11 12 13 14
15 16 17 18 19 20 21
22 23 24 25 26 27 28
29 30 31
```
APRIL
```
 S  M  T  W  T  F  S
             1  2  3  4
 5  6  7  8  9 10 11
12 13 14 15 16 17 18
19 20 21 22 23 24 25
26 27 28 29 30
```
MAY
```
 S  M  T  W  T  F  S
                1  2
 3  4  5  6  7  8  9
10 11 12 13 14 15 16
17 18 19 20 21 22 23
24 25 26 27 28 29 30
31
```
JUNE
```
 S  M  T  W  T  F  S
    1  2  3  4  5  6
 7  8  9 10 11 12 13
14 15 16 17 18 19 20
21 22 23 24 25 26 27
28 29 30
```
JULY
```
 S  M  T  W  T  F  S
             1  2  3  4
 5  6  7  8  9 10 11
12 13 14 15 16 17 18
19 20 21 22 23 24 25
26 27 28 29 30 31
```
AUGUST
```
 S  M  T  W  T  F  S
                   1
 2  3  4  5  6  7  8
 9 10 11 12 13 14 15
16 17 18 19 20 21 22
23 24 25 26 27 28 29
30 31
```
SEPTEMBER
```
 S  M  T  W  T  F  S
          1  2  3  4  5
 6  7  8  9 10 11 12
13 14 15 16 17 18 19
20 21 22 23 24 25 26
27 28 29 30
```
OCTOBER
```
 S  M  T  W  T  F  S
             1  2  3
 4  5  6  7  8  9 10
11 12 13 14 15 16 17
18 19 20 21 22 23 24
25 26 27 28 29 30 31
```
NOVEMBER
```
 S  M  T  W  T  F  S
 1  2  3  4  5  6  7
 8  9 10 11 12 13 14
15 16 17 18 19 20 21
22 23 24 25 26 27 28
29 30
```
DECEMBER
```
 S  M  T  W  T  F  S
          1  2  3  4  5
 6  7  8  9 10 11 12
13 14 15 16 17 18 19
20 21 22 23 24 25 26
27 28 29 30 31
```

6

JANUARY
```
 S  M  T  W  T  F  S
                1  2
 3  4  5  6  7  8  9
10 11 12 13 14 15 16
17 18 19 20 21 22 23
24 25 26 27 28 29 30
31
```
FEBRUARY
```
 S  M  T  W  T  F  S
    1  2  3  4  5  6
 7  8  9 10 11 12 13
14 15 16 17 18 19 20
21 22 23 24 25 26 27
28
```
MARCH
```
 S  M  T  W  T  F  S
    1  2  3  4  5  6
 7  8  9 10 11 12 13
14 15 16 17 18 19 20
21 22 23 24 25 26 27
28 29 30 31
```
APRIL
```
 S  M  T  W  T  F  S
             1  2  3
 4  5  6  7  8  9 10
11 12 13 14 15 16 17
18 19 20 21 22 23 24
25 26 27 28 29 30
```
MAY
```
 S  M  T  W  T  F  S
                   1
 2  3  4  5  6  7  8
 9 10 11 12 13 14 15
16 17 18 19 20 21 22
23 24 25 26 27 28 29
30 31
```
JUNE
```
 S  M  T  W  T  F  S
          1  2  3  4  5
 6  7  8  9 10 11 12
13 14 15 16 17 18 19
20 21 22 23 24 25 26
27 28 29 30
```
JULY
```
 S  M  T  W  T  F  S
             1  2  3
 4  5  6  7  8  9 10
11 12 13 14 15 16 17
18 19 20 21 22 23 24
25 26 27 28 29 30 31
```
AUGUST
```
 S  M  T  W  T  F  S
 1  2  3  4  5  6  7
 8  9 10 11 12 13 14
15 16 17 18 19 20 21
22 23 24 25 26 27 28
29 30 31
```
SEPTEMBER
```
 S  M  T  W  T  F  S
             1  2  3  4
 5  6  7  8  9 10 11
12 13 14 15 16 17 18
19 20 21 22 23 24 25
26 27 28 29 30
```
OCTOBER
```
 S  M  T  W  T  F  S
                1  2
 3  4  5  6  7  8  9
10 11 12 13 14 15 16
17 18 19 20 21 22 23
24 25 26 27 28 29 30
31
```
NOVEMBER
```
 S  M  T  W  T  F  S
    1  2  3  4  5  6
 7  8  9 10 11 12 13
14 15 16 17 18 19 20
21 22 23 24 25 26 27
28 29 30
```
DECEMBER
```
 S  M  T  W  T  F  S
             1  2  3  4
 5  6  7  8  9 10 11
12 13 14 15 16 17 18
19 20 21 22 23 24 25
26 27 28 29 30 31
```

7

JANUARY
```
 S  M  T  W  T  F  S
                   1
 2  3  4  5  6  7  8
 9 10 11 12 13 14 15
16 17 18 19 20 21 22
23 24 25 26 27 28 29
30 31
```
FEBRUARY
```
 S  M  T  W  T  F  S
          1  2  3  4  5
 6  7  8  9 10 11 12
13 14 15 16 17 18 19
20 21 22 23 24 25 26
27 28
```
MARCH
```
 S  M  T  W  T  F  S
          1  2  3  4  5
 6  7  8  9 10 11 12
13 14 15 16 17 18 19
20 21 22 23 24 25 26
27 28 29 30 31
```
APRIL
```
 S  M  T  W  T  F  S
                1  2
 3  4  5  6  7  8  9
10 11 12 13 14 15 16
17 18 19 20 21 22 23
24 25 26 27 28 29 30
```
MAY
```
 S  M  T  W  T  F  S
 1  2  3  4  5  6  7
 8  9 10 11 12 13 14
15 16 17 18 19 20 21
22 23 24 25 26 27 28
29 30 31
```
JUNE
```
 S  M  T  W  T  F  S
             1  2  3  4
 5  6  7  8  9 10 11
12 13 14 15 16 17 18
19 20 21 22 23 24 25
26 27 28 29 30
```
JULY
```
 S  M  T  W  T  F  S
                1  2
 3  4  5  6  7  8  9
10 11 12 13 14 15 16
17 18 19 20 21 22 23
24 25 26 27 28 29 30
31
```
AUGUST
```
 S  M  T  W  T  F  S
    1  2  3  4  5  6
 7  8  9 10 11 12 13
14 15 16 17 18 19 20
21 22 23 24 25 26 27
28 29 30 31
```
SEPTEMBER
```
 S  M  T  W  T  F  S
             1  2  3
 4  5  6  7  8  9 10
11 12 13 14 15 16 17
18 19 20 21 22 23 24
25 26 27 28 29 30
```
OCTOBER
```
 S  M  T  W  T  F  S
                   1
 2  3  4  5  6  7  8
 9 10 11 12 13 14 15
16 17 18 19 20 21 22
23 24 25 26 27 28 29
30 31
```
NOVEMBER
```
 S  M  T  W  T  F  S
          1  2  3  4  5
 6  7  8  9 10 11 12
13 14 15 16 17 18 19
20 21 22 23 24 25 26
27 28 29 30
```
DECEMBER
```
 S  M  T  W  T  F  S
             1  2  3
 4  5  6  7  8  9 10
11 12 13 14 15 16 17
18 19 20 21 22 23 24
25 26 27 28 29 30 31
```

8

JANUARY
```
 S  M  T  W  T  F  S
 1  2  3  4  5  6  7
 8  9 10 11 12 13 14
15 16 17 18 19 20 21
22 23 24 25 26 27 28
29 30 31
```
FEBRUARY
```
 S  M  T  W  T  F  S
             1  2  3  4
 5  6  7  8  9 10 11
12 13 14 15 16 17 18
19 20 21 22 23 24 25
26 27 28 29
```
MARCH
```
 S  M  T  W  T  F  S
             1  2  3
 4  5  6  7  8  9 10
11 12 13 14 15 16 17
18 19 20 21 22 23 24
25 26 27 28 29 30 31
```
APRIL
```
 S  M  T  W  T  F  S
 1  2  3  4  5  6  7
 8  9 10 11 12 13 14
15 16 17 18 19 20 21
22 23 24 25 26 27 28
29 30
```
MAY
```
 S  M  T  W  T  F  S
          1  2  3  4  5
 6  7  8  9 10 11 12
13 14 15 16 17 18 19
20 21 22 23 24 25 26
27 28 29 30 31
```
JUNE
```
 S  M  T  W  T  F  S
                1  2
 3  4  5  6  7  8  9
10 11 12 13 14 15 16
17 18 19 20 21 22 23
24 25 26 27 28 29 30
```
JULY
```
 S  M  T  W  T  F  S
 1  2  3  4  5  6  7
 8  9 10 11 12 13 14
15 16 17 18 19 20 21
22 23 24 25 26 27 28
29 30 31
```
AUGUST
```
 S  M  T  W  T  F  S
             1  2  3  4
 5  6  7  8  9 10 11
12 13 14 15 16 17 18
19 20 21 22 23 24 25
26 27 28 29 30 31
```
SEPTEMBER
```
 S  M  T  W  T  F  S
                   1
 2  3  4  5  6  7  8
 9 10 11 12 13 14 15
16 17 18 19 20 21 22
23 24 25 26 27 28 29
30
```
OCTOBER
```
 S  M  T  W  T  F  S
    1  2  3  4  5  6
 7  8  9 10 11 12 13
14 15 16 17 18 19 20
21 22 23 24 25 26 27
28 29 30 31
```
NOVEMBER
```
 S  M  T  W  T  F  S
             1  2  3
 4  5  6  7  8  9 10
11 12 13 14 15 16 17
18 19 20 21 22 23 24
25 26 27 28 29 30
```
DECEMBER
```
 S  M  T  W  T  F  S
                   1
 2  3  4  5  6  7  8
 9 10 11 12 13 14 15
16 17 18 19 20 21 22
23 24 25 26 27 28 29
30 31
```

9

JANUARY	FEBRUARY	MARCH
APRIL	MAY	JUNE
JULY	AUGUST	SEPTEMBER
OCTOBER	NOVEMBER	DECEMBER

10

JANUARY	FEBRUARY	MARCH
APRIL	MAY	JUNE
JULY	AUGUST	SEPTEMBER
OCTOBER	NOVEMBER	DECEMBER

11

JANUARY	FEBRUARY	MARCH
APRIL	MAY	JUNE
JULY	AUGUST	SEPTEMBER
OCTOBER	NOVEMBER	DECEMBER

12

JANUARY	FEBRUARY	MARCH
APRIL	MAY	JUNE
JULY	AUGUST	SEPTEMBER
OCTOBER	NOVEMBER	DECEMBER

13

JANUARY	FEBRUARY	MARCH
APRIL	MAY	JUNE
JULY	AUGUST	SEPTEMBER
OCTOBER	NOVEMBER	DECEMBER

14

JANUARY	FEBRUARY	MARCH
APRIL	MAY	JUNE
JULY	AUGUST	SEPTEMBER
OCTOBER	NOVEMBER	DECEMBER

Acknowledgments

First of all, there's Hannah Smart, who really, really is. Smart, that is.

Hannah is my eight-year-old editor who kindly took time out from reading C.L. Lewis' Narnia series to critique my first version of the sequel to *The Rachel Resistance.* "Leave out the cussing," Hannah wrote, "it might make kids cuss." She's right. So I did—even though that decision caused me to have to toss one hundred thirty pages and almost made me cuss myself!

Then there's Wendy Adler, former student (junior high English class), former babysitter (both my kids), and patient friend (if patience is, indeed, a virtue, this is the most virtuous woman who ever lived). Wendy kept me from throwing my computer through the window more times than one.

While this is a novel, so very many people kindly shared their true stories, their letters, their lives, that I fear I'll leave some out. But here goes: Jean Sims, sister of a brave young Marine; Ed O'Connor, brother of Joseph, who also served his country well; Kim David, the author of the teacher's guide to *The Rachel Resistance,* and extraordinary teacher and critic; Debbi Copp of the University of Oklahoma athletic department, who smoothed the way for my Rose Bowl connections; John McKinney, the guy who sprinkled the Oklahoma dirt between his toes; Kay Long and John Hinkle, who lived the California life of Paul Griggs themselves; Dennis King, Duke University archivist and author; Billie, Dennis, and Sister, my own personal cheering section; and, as always, Mattie and Louis, who put up with my retreating to the "Cave" for days at a time without protest. And finally, the information desk staff at the Norman Public Library, and David and Marilyn Todd, the best research staff and friends any writer has ever had.

Lone Scouts of America

The Lone Scouts of America organization (LSA) existed from 1915 until it became a division of Boys Scouts of America (BSA) in 1924. While based on the same ideals of dependability, initiative, and resourcefulness as the Boy Scouts, the LSA also emphasized independence and self-motivation. Through LSA, boys were helped to develop good manners, confidence, courage, leadership abilities, and the spirit of service, no matter how isolated their location. Thousands of boys became responsible citizens as a result of LSA.

From the start, *Lone Scout* magazine served as the link between founder and Chief Totem W.D. Boyce and the membership. Through its pages, Lone Scouts were provided requirements, general information, articles, stories, and input from the members. Eager to communicate with Chief Totem and fellow members, Lone Scouts began to write to and for the magazine. An awards program encouraged literary talent and gave recognition to those who submitted items worthy of publication in *Lone Scout*. A large percentage of the membership participated, and before long the majority of the magazine consisted of membership submittals.

—Victor P. Crain,
Lone Scout Foundation Trustee,
Lone Scout Memory Lodge Journal Editor,
and son of an LSA Lone Scout

[Author Harold Keith, to whom this book is dedicated, was a Lone Scout who went on to win the prestigious Newbery Medal for *Rifles for Watie*. When he spoke to schoolchildren, Mr. Keith always attributed his literary success to the fact that he had honed his skills writing for *Lone Scout* magazine as a youth.]

Glossary

B-17E—a WW II bomber plane.

Barker, Arrie—Ma Barker was a notorious woman in the 1930s. She was called "Old Lady Arrie Barker, Mother of Fred Barker" on reward posters distributed all over the Midwest. The mother-son duo was described on the reward posters as "Gangsters of the Kimes-Inman Gang of Oklahoma, Missouri, Kansas, and Texas."

Bryan, William Jennings—famous orator and politician who was involved in the famous Scopes "Monkey Trial."

cistern—a tank for catching and storing rainwater.

Cunningham, Glenn—Nicknamed "Kansas Ironman," Glenn was a track star who survived severe burns on his legs as a boy. He was one of the world's top middle-distance runners during the 1930s and won the prestigious Sullivan Award in 1933 as the nation's top athlete. He set a world one-mile record of 4:06 in 1934.

Daddy Warbucks—little Orphan Annie's guardian.

Dalton Gang and James Brothers—two sets of brothers who were infamous bank and train robbers.

enigma—puzzle; riddle.

erroneously—mistakenly.

feat—daring act of courage.

filibuster—a tactic used to delay something else from happening, usually through prolonged speech.

furlough—leave of absence from military duty.

Geneva Convention—The first Geneva Convention took place in 1864 with representatives of the major European powers in attendance. It established the neutrality of ambulances, hospitals, chaplains, and others engaged in caring for the sick and wounded during warfare. All persons employed in such service are required to wear a Geneva cross—red cross on a white background—as a sign of their office.

German saboteurs—In June of 1942, eight German saboteurs landed in the United States, four in Long Island, New York, and four in Florida. They were captured by the FBI that same month. On August 3 all eight were found guilty. Six were electrocuted on August 8 in the District of Columbia jail. President Franklin Roosevelt commuted the sentences of the other two.

hand grenade—a weapon containing charges and a timed fuse which will explode after ignited, usually in about five seconds.

Hatfields and McCoys—two families in Kentucky and West Virginia who carried on a thirty-year bloody feud in the late 1800s.

highfalutin'—extra fancy; pretending to be something you are not.

incendiary bombs—bombs that set off fires when they explode.

Japanese detention camps—"A military zone that included about half of California, two-thirds of

Washington and Oregon, and less than half of Arizona was established March 3, 1942. All persons of Japanese descent were required to evacuate this area. About 110,000 Japanese and Japanese-Americans were housed in ten detention centers outside the military zone." (From *The Book of Presidents* by Tim Taylor.)

Kraut—colloquial term for sauerkraut; used during the war to mean the Germans.

Lazarus—biblical character who returned from the dead.

Midway Island—island in the Pacific Ocean between Hawaii and Japan.

odious—deserving of hatred; abhorred.

oppugner— one who fights with words instead of weapons.

pounding—a wedding shower where the guests present a gift of a pound of some kind of food to the bride and groom.

prevaricator—liar.

rationing—limiting the supply of some material.

Richter Scale—The Richter Magnitude Scale was developed in 1935 by Charles F. Richter of the California Institute of Technology as a mathematical device to measure the size of earthquakes.

smelling salts—a substance containing ammonia and a scent, used to revive someone who has fainted.

snooker—cheat; deceive.

soda clerk—drug store employee who made milkshakes, ice cream Sundays, frosted Cokes, etc.

speed limit—In May of 1942 the speed limit across the United States was reduced to 40 miles per hour to save gasoline. Later it was reduced to 35.

Steinbeck, John—well-known writer and author of *The Moon Is Down,* a novel about Norway under the rule of the Nazis.

teletypewriter—an electromechanical typewriter that either transmits or receives messages coded in electrical signals carried by telegraph or telephone wires.

Teletype—a trademark for a teletypewriter.

ten-cent store—also called a "five and dime" store because most of the merchandise was very economically priced.

triskaidekaphobia—fear of the number thirteen.

UPI (United Press International)—a newspaper wire service which picked up interesting articles from around the world and sold them to the papers who subscribed to their services.

V-mail—Letters written on special sheets of paper with glue along the sides so the single sheet formed both the letter and the envelope. The sheets were then photographed and transferred to microfilm for shipping, reducing the amount of space needed and therefore speeding up delivery time.

victory garden—vegetable and fruit gardens planted during the war.

War Time—On February 2, 1942, all the clocks in the United States were advanced one hour to save energy. This was a year-round form of Daylight Savings Time which did not end until September 30, 1945.